From the Ashes

# She Smiled

## JOAN HEPHZIBAH

Dave & Julie
Keep Smiling
J. Hephm

ISBN: 978-1-9162525-0-9

## DEDICATION

To those with questions; why did I have to go through all I did go through.

To the sweet memories of Mama Puerii and Grandpa O.

To my daughters, you bring out the best in mum.

## ACKNOWLEDGEMENTS

I would like to thank all those involved in sharing my vision.

All my editing team, for a great job of editing.

To all friends and family, my gratitude.

# FOREWORD

I have read with heightened interest in the dynamics of the life of Chloe. Every portion of this book keeps you in suspense as to what the next phase is. Each chapter of the book is loaded with sundry lessons and important values for parents grappling with the task of child-rearing. Everybody else, young and old would find values to learn. I consider this book would make an interesting addition to any library collection of books. Overall, the book inspires the reader to hang on with the hope that anyone can overcome even the most difficult situations and the darkest moments of life. Sit tight and enjoy this wonderful story about the life of Chloe.

Uche Udeochu, PhD Associate Professor of Chemistry University of Maryland Eastern Shore, USA.

# SETTING THE SCENE

*The tears streamed down, and I let them*
*flow as freely as they would, making of them*
*a pillow for my heart, on them, I rested.*
*Saint Augustine*

Comatose in hopeless rage, her body moved like a defended ghost. Her feeble hands turned the doorknob in grave pain. Chloe now in her forties sat on an old grey reclining chair in her garden, recalling the phases of her life. The clear Scottish cyan evening sky above her went unappreciated — Notable depicted by the despair in her eyes. Her feet twitched in the cool breeze left behind as summer tended the grass with its mild heat. The direct sunset that settled over her eyes added to the discomfort she was feeling. She was still a beautiful woman to admire.

Even though her usual vibrant skin was now dry and pale from a lack of sleep, she was desperate for rest. The trials of the past few months sped up taking their toll on her.

To Chloe, it felt like she was in a horrible winter season, feeling icy cold inside. Events she never dreamt she would experience had piled up on to her one after the other during the last few months. She was considering her relationship with the Saviour and her great personality.

"Is this what hell feels like?" Chloe wondered.

Her recriminations imaginations chased each other around and around in her head.

*"Why do I keep getting everything wrong? I believed I had it all figured out, my faith, my job, my family, and all my friends. I am a priceless Renaissance painting broken into pieces. Can I be put together again? I can't remember when last I heard the Saviour speak to me. I am in a dry and parched land."*

A call on her mobile interrupted her brain waves. Chloe looked at the caller ID.

*"Pastor Mark again? I can't deal with this anymore. I am losing it. I've gone from the feeling of desolation to the brink of suicide. If I don't show up in church again, the Pastor would come and visit me. I would have to go. I need to speak to someone. This feeling is killing me."*

She refused to take the call.

The next Sunday morning, she attended the fellowship. Even though she was operating on autopilot, she made efforts. Very little of the service registered, but it still left her feeling a little calmer.

Surprised and embarrassed, she stepped into Pastor's massive hug as she turned to leave. The embrace gave her a tiny glimpse of hope. That was all it took; Chloe could not control her tears any longer.

"Do you want to talk about it?" Pastor Mark asked. "You could speak to my wife if that would make you feel more comfortable," handing her a handkerchief.

"I… I think I want to speak to someone neutral. I am caught in a web and want to get out before it's too late," Chloe murmured, still shivering.

"I would introduce you to Ms Black. She is a great counsellor, and we would pray for you." He placed his hand on her shoulder.

On the day of her first appointment with the counsellor, Chloe stood outside the front of the office. Reluctant to go in. She knew that once she crossed this threshold, it would commit her. *For the first time, she must go back to her childhood to dig up the dark and undefined past. A part that was still defining her present.* Ms Black opened her door with a warm, welcoming smile.

"I saw you through the window, Ms," she said.

"Ms Chloe," she replied.

"I could see you were hesitating to knock, so I thought it might help. Welcome. Come in; take a seat. Would you like tea or coffee?"

Chloe still felt uncomfortable. Avoided eye contact as she stepped into the office. It was gloomy without being oppressive. She let out a sigh as she sat on the beautiful, coloured seat. The ambience of the room was appealing. The artistic decorations dotted around the room provided a sense of peace. A peace that she longed for desperately.

"I would prefer some water, thanks" Chloe replied, leaning back into the seat.

"Coming right up," said Ms Black, leaving the room. She returned within minutes and handed Chloe a long glass filled with cold water. She, at a snail's pace, sipped some as she watched Ms Black over the rim of the glass. Chloe settled into the seat without delay opposite her.

"I understand you might not be ready to discuss everything at the moment. But let me take you through how this would work...."

As Ms Black continued, Chloe's mind drifted off until it lost her in reflection. Trying to make sense of her life meant that she had unravelled the web that was strangling her.

Chloe must decide which doors to open, which exits to close. Possibly what to do with the rest of her life. Today, she started that process by opening up to someone she must pretend to trust.

✿ ✿ ✿

At the second meeting, after they had settled in their seats.

Ms Black said, "I know it is going to be a difficult task for you to talk. Most people I work with are reluctant to do so. I usually suggest that they narrated their experiences in the 'third person'. It might make it easier for you to face your fears and depression."

Chloe lifted her face, giving Ms Black a glimmer of a smile, revealing her beautiful dimples. Chloe relaxed a little more.

"Yes, I reason I could do that," she responded unruffled. She took a deep breath,

"It all began one evening in Ibadan, Nigeria, West

Africa, in 1978…"

## ODD CELEBRATION

*I praise you because I am fearfully and
wonderfully made; your works are wonderful;
I know that full well.*

Thank goodness! She has made it this far, Chloe is a year-old today! As the fourth child, birthday celebrations were not an expectation. Her mother, Ruth (or Mama Joe as the children called her) was under constant pressure. She had to raise the family on her own. Since their father, Richard (Papa Joe) was always absent. His drive was to make the success of his profession. Ruth's heartbeat elevated with every drop of rain touching down on the aluminium roof.

Peering through the window, she saw the rainbow beaming from the trees. Her reality was pallid as though she had never seen the sun.

Wishing her world could be as colourful as the rainbow. Mama Joe looked down at her daughter lying in her tiny baby cot. In hopelessness, she reached out to the wet towel. She sat on a stool to cool the high fever that was ravishing her ever so sick body. In tears, her nose runny, coughing in discomfort with inflamed eyes. Tears dripped down her cheeks as she contemplated her impossible situation.

"What can I do? If only I could take her place. Is there something I should have done that I have not done? Have I offended anyone that my baby should pay for it?"

She untied her wrapper to clean her nose a mixture of tears and mucus. It flooded like the stream outside her home.

From the rain flooding of her house in the middle of nowhere. To the absence of neighbours to reach out to her. There was so much to contend with around her. Her only blessed companions were the cool breeze: the evergreen trees and a stream flowing beside her home.

A constant quiet sound was soothing her soul. Her four children filled her world of loneliness. The children sauntered into the gloomy room when they heard her sobbing in tears.

Reaching out, Joe said, "Mama, Mama, Chloe would be all right. Why do you keep crying in sorrow? We don't want to lose you too." Their empathetic hands formed a circle that drew her in their full embrace.          Singing one of her favourite comfort songs:

> My children are my wealth; My children are my
> life; My children are my friends; My comfort
> from above."

The rhythm of the song soon lit up the room like a

candlelight in a dark room, glimpsed smiles returned to Mama Joe's face. They watched their little sister comforted by their presence amidst her pain.

By sunset, Chloe's temperature had skyrocketed. She was getting pale. The spots had almost covered her entire tiny body, and she was breathing like mad.

With no way out, Mama Joe picked up Chloe's dying body. She was screaming her head off while pacing all over the house, yelling, "God! God! Help my baby. Don't take her away from me! My baby, my baby."

In her disturbed state, she picked up one of her Ankara wrappers and tied naked Chloe onto her back. She tried to figure out a way to keep her child alive.

She left the rest of the children in the care of Chloe's 10-year-old brother Joe. Mama Joe ran out of the house, down the path that leads away from home. She could hear the crickets making melancholic music. The untarred clay path was wet and muddy.

For every movement she took the dirty water splashed all over her. Thus, causing further distress to the baby. At the end of the path where it emerged near the road, she screamed,

"Taxi, taxi! Help! Help! Someone help, my baby is dying, Help!" but everywhere was as quiet as a graveyard. She kept crying.

"Please, God! Please help me." Chloe was shutting her eyes.

As she cried, her tiny little voice grew fainter with every passing second.

Moments later, an old car drove up. The sound of the vehicle blasted so loud that Chloe fainting eye sprouted open, with a loud cry like a 'this minute' born baby. The driver stopped and got out to see or investigate why Mama Joe was so agitated.

Seeing the distress in her eyes, he inquired how he could help. She recounted how she had noticed a few spots on her baby's body a few days earlier. Mama Joe narrated how things had progressed, bringing her close to death's door.

She wanted to get to the hospital without delay to save her beloved daughter. The driver rushed to open the dented door, escorted her in, and on the spur of the moment drove away.

The driver seemed undisturbed, watching her through the dashboard mirror. Tears rolled down her cheeks. She spoke in distress, cuddling her sobbing baby.

He responded in a subtle voice speaking pidgin English. "Madam make you no cry again. I think I know wetin dey do your pikin…e be like say na measles. If you allow me, I fit prescribe one shrub to you. Just cook am. Use am bathe your pikin. Make you give your pikin some of the water drink".

> "Madam don't cry. I know what is happening to
> your child. I sense its measles. I would prescribe one
> leaf to you, cook it, give her some to drink and use
> the rest for bathing her, including the leaves."

Speechless at first, Chloe's mother spoke up at the top of your voice.

"From where I may get the leaves?"

She was desperate to try anything that would bring her child back to good health. The driver parked nearby. After about five minutes, he came back with what looked like a bunch of weeds.

Handing it over to Chloe's mother, he said, "Madam your pikin no go die, just do as I say immediately."

10

"Madam, your child, would not die; do as I have
told you immediately."

Despite the driver's native herbal prescription,
something told Ruth that she still needed to go to the
hospital. They arrived at the hospital; the torturous
journey would be a waste of time.

There was no doctor on call, and all the nurse did was
to give Chloe some painkillers. They relieved Mama Joe
that her baby was in safe hands. Nevertheless, trepidation
filled her every pore as thoughts of the unknown plagued
her.

Finally, the doctor arrived, confirmed that the child was
suffering from measles. It was at its critical stage. "Chloe
could have died if you had not brought your baby in
now," the doctor said.

They administered medication as a matter of urgency,
to bring Chloe's temperature down. They stayed for a few
hours to make sure that her body heat came down to the
minimum acceptable level before they headed back home.

The doctor advised of the possibility of side effects
because of the late diagnosis and treatment. Ruth
determined to give the older man's herbal prescription a
trial to make sure that her daughter got well.

Mama Joe infused the herbs and bathed Chloe in the
herbal fusion as directed by the taxi driver. Within three
days, she was back to normal health.

The herbal infusion, coupled with the hospital
medications worked. It excited the children to have their
sister back in good health. They loved her smiles and how
she drew with joy to their comfort songs. Her most
exciting move was rattling her feet like a baby's toy when
she was excited.

The sad days faded away bit by bit and, they soon
forgot she was once gravely ill. Chloe grew from strength
to strength until she could take her first step.

Mama Joe's mind still rattled by the doctor's last word. It beats like the drums of the masquerade, "Possible of side effects."

A few months after Chloe developed a series of ear infections. The infections led to an episode of bronchitis. She became a fragile little child fighting for her life with each hit of another illness.

By the time she entered the troubled toddler age of three, she had taken ill again. This time, they diagnosed it early to be pneumonia. Chloe became the centre of magnetism of the family. She needed constant devotion, assurance, and care.

Sarah, her immediate sister, perceived the attention as favouritism, brewing a troubled rivalry. Though Chloe was sickly, she was strong-willed. Mama Joe interpreted her wilfulness as strength against all the odds. Notably, this first few years of her life. To Sarah, it is the only reason she can't wait to get rid of her.

Why does she always have all the of Mama's attention? Do I have to make myself sick to get mother on my right side? Questions turned into adverse reactions against Chloe. Joe was very protective.

He treasured Chloe as the 'almost lost' sister, however, like acid, this added to Sarah's envious wounds. Josh, the other brother, was indifferent. An equal opportunity guy in any argument, often settling scores among his sisters.

One crazy afternoon, a playtime with Sarah put Chloe in danger. Mama Joe had left the house for some errands for her father. Joe was the 'responsible adult' in charge of all the children.

He left the girls to play by themselves while he dashed off with Josh. Embroiled in a game of football the boys forgot all about the girls. The fun did not last long, as till they heard an ear-splitting cry at the back of the house. It was an unmistakable cry of a distinct voice – Chloe.

The boys recalled the backyard was out of bounds for the girls. Mama Joe only allowed them to feed the chicken alone. Occasionally, Sarah would request to help. How and why in the world was Chloe's voice blasting like a broken record player from the back of the house.

Joe ran faster than his legs could carry him to the source of the noise. In the meantime, Josh tried to dispose of any evidence of their distractive activities.

Joe held back his anger at the sight of Sarah's hands crossed against her chest.

"What have you done to her?" He shouted, pushing her away from the front of the cage. Sarah's countenance changed with tears in the eyes, creating an innocent display.

"I don't know how the incident happened," she protested.

Joe shouted out to Josh, "Josh! Josh, please bring a bowl of water. Chloe's hurt!"

His immediate action was to drag Chloe out of the cage. The whole poultry was in a panic. The frightened animals ran helter-skelter creating a complete pandemonium scene. Joe bent and cuddled Chloe into his hands as a foot bled.

In a flash, Josh arrived at the scene of the accident with a bowl of water. Joe was sitting on the floor by the entrance of the cage. He carried the sobbing Chloe on his bosom, which gave her the comfort she so much needed.

As her cry subsided, he took the towel from Josh's troubled face who knelt beside him. Joe, with his gentle personality, cleaned the wound with water to ease the bleeding.

Facing Josh, he said, "Do you know where Mama keeps the bandage?"

"I do," responded Sarah, another bid to express her support.

Minimising eye contact with her while staring at Josh, Joe replied, "Go with her and get it. We need to do something, or she would keep bleeding."

Rather than responding to the direction of Sarah's steps into the house, Josh shocked his feet unto the red sand underneath him.

Retrieving his shaking voice in tears, he replied, "Joe, please, let's call Papa. He would still be in the office. We can't contact Mama..."

While still speaking, Sarah returned to find an exacerbated little girl with her brother. Chloe was crying with mucus all over her face, with Josh pacifying her.

"Sorry, Chloe, sorry baby, you would be fine."
Joe looked at Sarah with no emotion on his face.
Sarah pleaded.

"I am sorry."

"You are sorry for what?" Josh responded in anger. "Didn't you do this?" he shouted at Sarah.

Sensing the anger in Josh's tone, Sarah dropped the bandage and ran into the house.

With blood still dripping from the centre of her right foot, Joe wrapped the bandage on it. He carried Chloe into the house and offered her a cup of Choco Milo drink.

Mama Joe arrived after the drama to find a sleeping Chloe with a rough bandage on her leg. She screamed, "What did you do to my baby?"

Joe rushed out of his room and took full responsibilities for the part he played.

Mama was not going to take it lightly. She pulled Sarah into the room by her ears.

"What did you do to my baby? I know you are the one responsible for this? You are the only one, always upset with her. Sarah! What did you do to her?"

Sarah stood frozen to the floor while Josh came to her rescue. He explained that Chloe followed Sarah to pick eggs.

She backed the cage to arrange the eggs into the basket. In amazement, she turned her back at Chloe, who by chance stepped on the gate of the enclosure. The extended wire on the cage speared into her leg.

Make a clean breast; the story was believable. Sarah was afraid that the truth might come to light. She knew that she would be disciplined further, for her action if her mother gets to find out the truth.

Hence, to avoid punishment, Sarah decided that the fact would have to die with her. She led Chloe, a gullible toddler, to show her the chickens. Chloe followed her to enjoy the adventure in her naivety.

Sarah had wicked intention toward Chloe. She pushed her into the cage to frighten her at the entrance of the gate. Unfortunately, in a panic to escape from the animals, one of the barbed wires speared her feet. The healing process left a large scar on Chloe's right foot. Each sighting of the injury, she watched in regret.

Sarah regretted her actions. She resolved to treat her little sister better.

✿ ✿ ✿

It wasn't long before they would discover a more significant issue. The measles would have a lifelong effect on little Chloe.

All these events increased tensions amidst family dynamics. Once Chloe started teething, her mother noticed her teeth were yellowish (discoloured). Instead of the regular pearly white.

Besides, Chloe would complain of relentless eye aches.

A visit to the hospital and a series of medical tests confirmed Mama Joe's greatest fears. The bout of measles had affected her sight and teeth.

Little Chloe endured constant medical check-ups. Mondays to the eye clinic, Fridays to the dentist every week for years. The visits changed how Chloe saw herself - the weak one, deformed for the rest of her life.

# ENCOUNTER WITH SELF

*In their hearts,' humans plan their course,*
*but the Lord establishes their steps.*

Expressing her emotions to others was an uphill task for a five-year-old Chloe. Various mood swings that followed the many visits to the hospital. They, against her will, helped her to see herself as unlovable. Fear, anticipation, hope that they would fix things — the disappointment when they weren't. Impatience and relief on the double chased each other around and around until she got home. Into the bargain, she felt rejected.

A result of her father's insistence that Chloe must not wear her prescription eyeglasses. He said that she was too young.

"Too young," she chewed over to herself, puzzled.

"I don't understand, Papa Joe, why I am too young?" She looked into his eyes while crying, "Papa, my eyes hurt; my teeth ache all the time."

"Wearing eyeglasses would define you and destroy your eyes;" he said firmly. Papa Joe walked away without looking back. What Chloe didn't know was that his resistance. Resulted from the fact that he detested using glasses himself.

As a little girl, Chloe wondered why her father didn't love her.

She recounted, *"Do my constant hospital visits not bother him. Does it make me less of a child compared to my other siblings? I shouldn't have been born! Did it have something to do with the five-year age gap between my older sister and me? It could be Dad never wanted me considering the age gap?"*

In those days, that was a significant age gap between siblings. One or two years was considered ideal.

Nevertheless, she pushed aside those evil perceptions. When she remembered that life was worth living with a gentle and caring Mama Joe, she is always willing to listen and comfort her.

Chloe's self-awareness grew much like the rising of the sun to light up the world. Chloe knew she was an adorable little girl, with smiles like the light of the morning. There was a lack of understanding of her completeness.

She often compared herself to her siblings. She in perpetuity did draw into dimming darkness of self-loathing, like the sunset.

Chloe was five years old when she had the first corrective surgery for her eyes. Her operation was followed by her treatment to strengthen her weak gums.

Mama Joe had tried to comfort her, even though the medical procedures were beyond her comprehension or mental ability. Mama Joe not formally educated, but she was the most robust support Chloe had to carry her through.

The appointment to determine if surgery would be an option was on a cold, dry, and dusty harmattan morning.

Apart from the unbearable weather, Papa Joe's driver was late. The combination of events meant Chloe and her mother arrived late for their appointment. The town's University Medical Centre was the only well-equipped teaching hospital. In the country of about 100 million people. They referred people from all over.

An appointment did not guarantee the doctor's examination. Though the patients have set nominated time, the sick were attended to on a 'first come, first served' basis.

Being attended to by the doctors depends on the connections, one had within the hospital. There was always a possibility that a nine am appointment might mean they would not attend to a patient until almost the close of the day.

The hospital departments operated an 'open clinic' policy. Regardless of how dangerous the degree an ailment might be. Each week, they treated some gruesome eye diseases presented before Chloe.

The sight of the clinic was a trauma for a frail mind. There was a stench in the air rising from the combination of foul-smelling sores. The scene was often a mixture of the horrid smell and with the odour of the department's disinfectants.

The view and smell created an unpleasant bitter-sweet

childhood experience. All these offensive scenes attacked the girl's senses, making Chloe sicker than she felt. It was puzzling and incomprehensible for her young age. Chloe felt torn between pain and comfort.

Mama Joe and Chloe arrived at the hospital two hours late for her appointment at the eye clinic. The environment was brimming like a ton of bricks with ill patients. Mama Joe had to send the driver to bring her husband to speed up the process.

Chloe shivered as she waited for the driver to return. Papa Joe was famous around the hospital. Once he arrived, all the doors that had shut to Mama Joe flew open, and other patients appointment times had to wait.

Papa Joe walked into the consultant's office, exchanging pleasantries. The doctor at once ushered Chloe and her mother into his office.

Sometimes, Chloe imagined Papa Joe as the *'proud superman'* who could solve any problem. Once he left, they treated her Mama Joe otherwise. 'Belittled' was the best description of how Chloe imagined that her mother felt, though she did not express her displeasure.

The doctor who examined Chloe was one of the well-known consultants. Admitting, he was pleasant; she feared his masculinity. He reminded her of her father, and she held on to Mama Joe's hand with a terrifying grip.

Chloe went through a prolonged examination of her medical records and scans. The doctor recommended corrective surgery for chronic astigmatism resulting from the measles. But the short-sightedness observed she inherited from her father.

Her Papa Joe was well-off enough to afford the Radial Keratotomy treatment, although the advanced medical procedure was not available. An invention by a Japanese surgeon in the late 70s.

The consultant had recently returned to Africa from

overseas. He of late, trained in this procedure. Chloe would be one of his clinical trials; the treatment would be an experiment.

The process required small cuts on the surface of the cornea to change its shape. They set a date for the surgery, and they returned home.

❁ ❁ ❁

The night before the surgery, Chloe woke up with a nightmare screaming,

"My eyes, my eyes. Help, Mama, Help!"

Mama Joe ran into the darkroom she shared with her sister. She cuddled her as she laid her hands on her child's eyes.

Praying, she whispered, "God Help me. Keep my daughter in your care and stop this awful pain."

Chloe held on to her mother. Her breath was heavy as she remembered the details of the dream, where she lost her sight. Chloe expressed her anxiety about the surgery.

"I don't want to go to the hospital, Mama." She cried.

"You would be fine. You are a strong child. I would be with you." Mama Joe spoke decisively, wiping away her tears.

The surgery was not as painful as Chloe had feared. After three hours, they transferred her to the children's recovery wing, where she would have to remain for two days.

Chloe's father influenced the clinical decisions for her not to stay in the hospital to recover. She returned home with mandatory daily and weekly follow-ups.

Chloe became a regular face at the clinic for her weekly check-up and dressing appointments. They nicknamed her 'Smile and Shy' because even though she was pleasant.

She was a shy little girl who was always hiding behind Mama Joe skirt. At one of her appointments, a few months after the surgery. The doctor discovered that the operation had not corrected the condition.

The only recommendation he could make was for her to use glasses as a corrective measure. In the interim, she would be on medication until a better medical procedure was available.

It was no different at the dental clinic. Chloe had horrifying experiences as they tried to rectify her weak gums. Resulting from the 'periodontal disease' she had suffered.

# ENCOUNTERS WITH OTHERS

*Do to others as you would have them do to you.*

Chloe woke up and jumped out of bed. She hurried to the window; She pulled the curtains apart, smiling back to the radiated beam of the morning light flooding into her room.

"It would be a joyful day! Mama always tells me to start my day on a joyful note."

Words, which were more like seeds dropped on rocky places in her heart. It excited Chloe to start school like her older siblings.

But she had to go to a different school from her
siblings. Papa Joe decided she would attend an
independent religious school. They carved the institution
out of a well-established branch. Renamed called
Precious Infant Nursery. Chloe never had a reason to
consider herself different from others. Not until she
arrived at the centre of learning.

Chloe leaned on the window from the rear seat where
she sat with her father. As the car pulled up to the school,
she watched the wind blow the trees lining the road
leading to the school. Chloe felt great delight.

*"My first impression is not bad after all",* she echoed.
Chloe watched the children walking into school with their
parents.

"Perchance I would be friends with one of these kids,"
she pondered.

As the driver drove through the school gate, she felt
excited. It surprised her at how exquisitely designed the
school was.

Two semi-circular buildings joined the central block,
which was the administrative office.

"There are lots of trees to climb, and the playground is
tempting," Chloe reflected.

Climbing trees at home were one of Chloe's favourite
fun activities. She walked towards the administrative
office, holding Papa Joe's hands. Chloe tried to count the
number of classes she could see.

The school administrator, with enthusiasm, welcomed
them and led them to the headmaster's office. Papa Joe
handed over Chloe to Mrs Martins, the head-teacher.
Chloe felt disconnected in an instance from familiarity.
She began to cry and pleaded to go back home. Mrs
Martins assured him that Chloe was in safe hands. She
gave Chloe a motherly embrace to feel better. Chloe was
led to her class after her father left.

Mr Umor, her class teacher, introduced her to the rest of the pupils. In class, she felt uncomfortable wishing Mama Joe was with her to save the day. At break time, Chloe felt different. The other students questioned and laughed at her physical appearance. In her innocence, Chloe had a brain wave that school would accommodate her like home. She was, yet, shaken by her experience on her first day of primary school.

The children surrounded her one afternoon and bombarded her with many questions. One of them asked,

"Why do you look like this, and why is your sight like that? Can you see at all?". Another one,

"Whoop! I never knew people could be born with different colours of teeth." Another one added,

"I know of only white teeth. Why is your own yellow, golden, brown?"

"What is the colour?" another yelled!
Chloe felt her head spinning in a circle, trying to make sense of their cruel words to her.

Chloe, unable to handle all the questions, waves of laughter and yelling, bust out crying. She ran under a tree at the farthest corner of the playground. There was no point reporting to the teacher; she felt awkward around him.

The spot soon became her cosy corner where she played by herself. As the days, months and years went by; she often wondered why the kids were so mean towards her, especially the girls.

Even though Chloe was a bright kid, most times, she would refuse to speak straight away. To prevent others from laughing on seeing her teeth. The constant bullying made her feel horrible about herself. Making new friends was the last thing on her mind. She little by little grew to be by herself, withdrawing to a safe place.     Her constant pondering was, *"Who will, in reality, be my friend apart from Mama Joe and my siblings?"*

Chloe soon noticed that some boys were nicer than the girls. They reached out to play with her sometimes when the crowd was not watching. She concluded that boys were easier to get along with than girls. An idea that in silence, directed the tenderness and relationship she kept as she grew up.

She found it easier to talk to boys. They had questions like the other kids, but the subjects did not create a barrier to their playtime.

Mr Umor, her class teacher, usually picked on her. Especially during the mental mathematics and general knowledge periods. School caused Chloe more distress and unexplainable shame. Feelings she could not express to her family.

"It could be that I am only weak. Will my loved ones not question why I must feel this way?" she often asked herself.

"You are perfect," her lovely big brother Joe often said. But will he ever understand it was a different playing field in school?

Chloe avoided conversations about being different. She allowed her sense of inferiority to pull her into the depth of withdrawal. The deficiency faded her inner beauty. Her physical charm was irresistible.

She was growing up to be one of the most beautiful, engaging little girls that ever existed. With her ebony complexion, an oval face, big brown eyes and a pair of dimples, it was impossible to stop gazing at her.

When she smiled, she had such a bright glow in her eyes that healed the weary soul. She was an admirable child, yet it drained her little heart of joy and full of anger.

✿ ✿ ✿

One morning, during the usual multiplication quiz. Chloe, too shy to speak froze and forgot to answer the question. Her mind was far away in her wonderland. The lashing stroke of the paddle she felt on her shoulder, interrupted her brainwaves.

She let out a scream, and the rest of the class burst out laughing at the top of their voice. Moments later, the sound of her teacher kept ringing in her mind.

"Stupid girl, you would not listen in class, you and your golden teeth! I cannot imagine who would marry such a girl with a golden set of teeth," he continued yelling.

"Normal children have white teeth; you came to the world with yellow teeth."

The rest of the class continued in an uproar, joining the teacher to laugh. Some children made fingering gestures towards her. Other classmates started making individual distasteful comments.

Soon the classwork focused on her. Shame ravished her entire being; she wanted the earth to open straight away and swallow her up. Her whole body froze.

"Could anything be worse than this?" she asked herself.

Chloe felt bullied, helpless and unwanted on the surface of the earth. For the rest of the day, Chloe cried herself into a frenzy. The school called her parents to pick her up as she had become unwell. One of Papa Joe's workers picked her up from school. Mama Joe, distraught at the state in which Chloe's teacher, had left her precious daughter. In anger, Mama Joe paced up and down like an angry lioness. Lashing out

"How could he! How could he do this? Without caring for my child's emotional and mental well-being."

The next morning, Chloe's mother took her daughter to school. She was heading straight to the headteacher's office. Mama Joe stormed past the Administrator's office to express her disappointment.     "Mr Umor's had maltreated and harassed my daughter."

Mama Joe exclaimed at the sight of Mrs Martins. The head-teacher calmed Chloe's mother down and expressed her sincere apologies. At the spur of the moment, the head-teacher made a promise. The school would not tolerate bullying. She would take actions to rectify the situation.

"My action," she said, "Would serve as a precedent in the school that such behaviour would not be stomached."

Chloe stayed away from school for five days. When she returned, it seemed Mrs Martins had served justice. News had spread around the school, that the headmistress had dismissed the teacher. Because of the poison, he spewed at Chloe, crushing her heart. Moreover, Chloe knew it had done the damage, even though her mother had stood up for her.

Also, though the loving voices of her brothers rang in her ears, reminding her, she is the most beautiful girl in the world. It wasn't enough; a scare had already being etched on the walls of her heart.

Deep down, Chloe questioned her six-year-old self,

*"Am I great enough? Will my teeth forever disqualify me from having my Prince Charming, as Mr Umor said?"*

She needed some reassurance from the only man in her life, Papa Joe, a reflection of her future husband. Her father was far from her reach.

*"Did he in fact care if I existed,"* Chloe wondered. Constant tension prevailed in their home. The attention she needed would never come from her father. She finally caught the attention of an unusual friend; a boy who was about four years older than her.

# CURIOUS – WHO AM I

*Your eyes will see strange sights, and
your mind will imagine confusing things.*

"Chloe! Chloe, it's time to go to work," called her father as he headed toward the front door.

It was the holidays, and all Papa Joe's children worked in the office. Papa said it was his way of introducing them to the business and trying to develop their work ethic. He was a stickler for things like that. Learning the trade was not likely to be the critical interest of a six-year-old, but she still had to go.

Chloe spent most of the day playing with neighbours and other workers' children. Many of them went to work with their parents during the school holidays.

Often the kids played close to the busy road. It was easy to take the uncalculated risk. Chloe knew Mama Joe had instructed her otherwise. The girls played skipping robes on the busy road and only moved at the horn of an ongoing vehicle.

The boys played with old worn-out tyres or a pre-determined fighting contest. The winner would be crown, a short-lived leader of the street gang.

Others make circles with hands clapping games accompanied by folks' songs. Chloe enjoyed playing with sand, which was the epic game.

Girls would draw lines on the sands and hops in between the space until a winner emerges. Chloe preferred playing with the boys, and she returned to the office dirty.

Whenever she was not taking a risk like the other kids, she watched other from afar. On the streets, little children like herself hawked a good deal of produce. They would be calling out for potential buyers along their route. Items ranged from food, snacks, such as boiled groundnuts.

Boiled groundnuts were one of her favourite meals. Papa Joe allowed her groundnuts if she behaved herself in the office — others hawked soaps and washing powder. The kids were hunger looking, tired and unhappy.

Two of such children took her attention. She imagined in her head; they were sent out by their wicked stepmother. Images of little Cinderella and her stepmother played out in her mind. The kids appeared unkempt and had no shoes.

The older child wore an old slipper stitched all over while the back was chipped off. Tattered clothes were trademarks of street kids, yet they had to sell their products. *"They even seem to live on the street,"* Chloe contemplated. She would imagine herself in their shoes.

At home, Chloe would imitate the kids by hawking her toys to her siblings, and they would laugh at her. She wanted to experience what it would be like to hawk on the street. Mama Joe reminded them that all fingers were not equal. It privileged her children to have all they wanted. Other kids had to work for every single meal; at times, she had to beg them before they ate. Her mother's words sounded like a distance lighting frequency to the ears of Chloe, the picker eater.

Papa Joe's factory was a vast building situated in a noisy residential area, inhabited by the middle-class families. Mokola was the first area with a layout ward, created by the colonial administration. It lies in direct connection with the University of Ibadan campus and Bodija to the East.

It was about an hour drive away from home. Towards the West is Dugbe, Agugu and Yemetu, leading to the slum area of the city. The street to the factory had a significant intersection zone to several regions of the city. The major crossway gave access to the city's main university teaching hospital: the famous Agodi garden, the beautiful botanical garden to the North and the busy market.

The southern part of his factory was "Sabo" the Northerners speaking parts of the city. Chloe's interests from Sabo was the Northern sweet called "Taba-Taba and Dankwa." Taba-Taba was a sweet savouring coloured hard sugar sweet. It left a trademark on the eater's tongue based on the colour of the delicacy eaten. Dankwa was a healthy version made of roasted and blended peanut and cornmeal.

Whenever she was well-behaved on the way from school, enroute from Sabo, Papa Joe's workers would buy some of these delicacies for her. Papa Joe's business blossom, it was located in the central part of the city.

It was a three-storey building — the loft was the storage of harmful chemicals stacked on top of each other. The sales department was on the ground floor. The administrative offices were on the first and manufacturing layout on the second floor.

One of Chloe's regular playmates was John, a nephew of one of Papa Joe's workers. John was a thin, fair-skinned, dull, pale-faced young boy; like a diluted milky coffee. He was four years older in age. On this holiday, as Chloe played with John, she asked,

*"What's the difference between a boy and a girl?"*

It was a question that started brewing at school. Chloe observed how both genders interacted with her in different ways. Playing with other kids on the street intensified her curiosity to find out.

She wanted to explore and understand the differences. Sometimes, she in secret followed the boys' urinating on the road.

"Why do they stand, and I have to crouch to pee?" she scrutinised.

She avoided a label of indecency. Besides, her curiosity and the sensitivity on a tabooed subject did not help. Chloe felt she could not even discuss this with her mother or her older brothers. Thus, she devised a plan to find out for herself.

The opportunity soon came. She found some pornography magazines in the back corner of the loft, among some stuff that she assumed belonged to Papa Joe's workers. Chloe, on the sly, started reading them.

*"Ikebe Super,"* a cartoon magazine that featured sexual activities between the opposite sexes. At first, it was awkward, but she soon got used to the feeling. She found a hiding place near a skylight.

The ray of light provided better brightness to digest the images portrayed in the magazines. It was better than the red light that all the time burned in an otherwise dark space. Unknown to her, John was also in private viewing *"Ikebe Super"* magazines.

Chloe was in her hiding place behind the boxes in the loft when John sneaked up on her. During the last three weeks of the holiday. They'd found each other out by coincidence.

"Did you take that from the loft?" John queried Chloe.

"Did you too?" asked Chloe, looking down like a thief caught in action.

"I don't want Mama Joe to know I read them. I don't think she likes them," she continued, still looking guilty.

"I know. It'll be our little secret." John replied, giving her a mischievous grin.

"I heard your mother telling your uncles never to bring them to the office. They seem to bring them in. Good for us," he added, giggling as if he won a trophy by the sudden revelation.

They both agreed that this would be their meeting place. They hatched a plan to view the cartoons together.

Deep down, Chloe knew there was something wrong about it. She did it behind closed doors and didn't want her family to know about it. Chloe felt it satisfied her curiosity.

She found that it drove her to a constant need, to explore what her senses craved for, from the cartoons.

One afternoon, Chloe, John and some other children, feeling bored, played in the loft. As a rule, the attic was a no-go-area for kids. Luckily for the children, there were no scheduled deliveries for that day. The loft had an awful odour from the various chemicals used in the factory.

Usually, there is a red bulb providing light to reduce the intensity of darkness in the room. That afternoon someone had turned the light off. The children didn't want to alert the adults to their whereabouts by turning it on.

As the children sneaked up into the loft, Chloe heard her mother. She turned up, unannounced to see Papa Joe. She reminded one of the staff members not to permit the children in the loft.

An instruction heeded by all the staff. John, being the oldest, led the children up the stairs inconspicuously. Chloe raised the small curtains in the darkroom to let in some rays of light.

The darken smell in the room assailed her senses. A usual occurrence, when she came up there to read in the loft, the other children gasped as it hit them. After a while, they forgot about it as they relished the feeling of breaking the rules. They knew they could not be there but stayed in the loft, all the same.

Chloe didn't realise that John had a particular motive. His selection of the attic as their play area that afternoon. It became apparent, though when he suggested they all play the game of "mummies and daddies."

The game sounded cool to Chloe's ears. Her intense curiosity and her recent interactions with the boys made her play along. She was, however, naive about the details of the game.

John assigned himself to play Daddy and Chloe to play Mummy. They allocated the other children the roles of being their children.

The game went on undisturbed for a little while until John decided that they needed to take it to the next level. With the other children watching, John and Chloe started by making eye contact. They moved closer together and started to hug each other as they had seen in the magazines.

They kept hugging each other, running their hands up and down each other's bodies. Chloe could hear the other children giggling in the background. They were egged on by the children's giggles.

John whispered that they should both pull down their pants to make the game even more realistic. Chloe complied without taking her eyes off John's face. John's hands continued to move over her body. John held her forcefully against him until he touched her 'nether regions'.

Out of the blue, she felt a grave violation. The sense she felt was not in truth the feeling she expected. Chloe felt stupid and dirty, knowing that somehow, her childhood innocence was forever lost.

Chloe broke away from John. Picking up her pants, she ran out of the loft. Chloe left the other children behind in dumb-founded silence. She was falling over some boxes in the hallway as if there was an imminent danger. Chloe little legs ran for a safe place.

She heard Mama Joe call out,

"Who is there! What are you doing there!"

Chloe refused to answer her mother's call. She escaped to the playroom, crawling under the table with fear and trembling.

*"Mama must not find out what happened in the past few minutes! What have I done!"* she cried like a ghost to herself?

*"I had expected that there would have been a feeling of satisfaction. My ever-longing curiosity! But where is it?"* Chloe quizzed herself. *"But this hadn't been the case. No, it was far from the reality I was expecting,"* she blamed herself.

Chloe felt so ashamed of her actions. Pulling up her pants, she felt the need to have a bath; a sick feeling engulfed her for what she had done.

*"There's no one I can tell who would understand. I went along with it. It's all my fault!"* Chloe told herself time and again.

She finally emerged from under the table when her mother came looking for her.

"Chloe, it's time to go home," Mama Joe announced. She pretended that she had been cooking and under the table had been her make-believe kitchen.

✿ ✿ ✿

Chloe knew that if anyone found out what had happened, she would be in trouble. She crossed the lines of the traditional expectations of a six-year-old girl. She made sure that she didn't go anywhere where she might meet John again.

Luckily for her, John's visit was over the following week. Chloe prayed that she would never set eyes on his face for the rest of her life. A search that began so intriguing now seemed to be monstrous.

She knew that what they had done was an abomination to her family's deep cultural and religious beliefs. The guilt of exploring that uncharted territory caused her to withdraw deeper. Deeper into the abyss of self-loathing. It was making her lonelier than she already felt.

She didn't understand that her emotional awareness was a mix of the sheer lack of a father's love. And, a need to seek love with anyone who could replace it. She felt less worthy and inferior, and so couldn't comprehend what true friendship would be.

Chloe's guilt pulled her inward; the rejection that ripped her heart in shreds left a mark on her. She vowed never to allow anyone, especially boys, got close to her body. Except for her prince charming (according to the latest book, 'Cinderella' she recently read).

*"I would allow no one to make me feel such pain again,"* as she constructed rigid walls around her heart. She fed her ugly imaginations daily. Making friends became very difficult because of her experience with John.

Chloe examined the world through her little glass of hurts and gross impossibility. She couldn't deal with the fragments of her fragile heart; neither did she open up to anyone.

Nothing prepared her for the journey. Especially the relationships that walked through her life.

# DID I DO THAT!

*Let them praise his name with dancing and
make music to him with timbrel and harp.*

Did Papa Joe reasonably leave me alone at the party? Or it could be he forgot about me? Ideas ran through Chloe's mind as she sat on the sofa in her father's friend house.

Aunty Banks was one of Papa's close friends and business associates. She had a large house in an exclusive area in the city. Papa Joe, however, built his home in the suburbs, for reasons best known to him.

It was Aunty Banks' son's wedding day. They had chosen Chloe to be one of the flower girls. It was Chloe's first wedding, and the whole experience was new to her. Hitherto, the wedding was over, and the evening was fast approaching. Chloe wondered why her father had not returned to take her home.

Papa Joe had dropped Chloe off early in the morning. The plan, she mulls over, was for him to pick her up from Aunty Banks' house after the wedding.

10-year-old, Chloe knew he had planned out the whole day for her; there was no need for her to make a fuss. Bimpe, one of the other flower girls, introduced herself to shy Chloe, as soon as Papa Joe left. As she held Chloe's hands, she walked into the house, by shank's pony, like a model.

Bimpe introduced Chloe to all who cared to listen. She swayed straight on, delighting in the attention she was receiving.

"Meet my beautiful friend Chloe, don't worry, she doesn't talk much. I met her today, and I know we would be best of friends."

Chloe trailed after her while Bimpe made the introductions.

*"She has reduced my workload,"* Chloe agreed, without protest, she greeted everyone as expected.

Her presentations went on until Bimpe came face to face with the maid of honour. She immediately raised her voice and shouted.

"Bimpe! Bimpe, didn't I tell you to stay in the room? Do you want us to be late? Do you know we still need to get to the bride's house?"

Bimpe, still holding Chloe's hand, stood still, looking as if she had seen a ghost, her eyes fixed on the maid of honour.

"Naughty girl, always talking, non-stop! Who asked you to be Chloe's mouthpiece? You would explain to your mother later," the lady continued.

Chloe felt sorry for Bimpe but wished she could be as expressive as she was. Bimpe and Chloe walked in silence behind the maid of honour. She led them to the car and the driver waiting outside, in the compound.

Arriving at the bride's house ten minutes later, they ushered them into inside. Conceding not as big as Aunty Banks, the house was busy.

Everyone shouted over each other while getting ready for the wedding. Outside, several women were cooking, preparing the food.

The cooking was for the wedding reception and the evening party at the bride's house. The aroma was breathtaking. Chloe longed for some delightful cuisine as her stomach rumbled. Even though she knew she was not a great eater.

The smells reminded Chloe that some cooking was also happening in the groom's house.

*"Do they have to cook another way in both family houses? Who would eat all the food? Will they be inviting the whole town to the party?"*

Chloe had never experienced such a massive party in her ten years of existence. She soon began to get excited, allowing her to forget her shyness and enjoy the fun.

Everyone loved her dress; she felt like a goddess! Chloe wore a lovely petite white dress with her hair decorated with pink and white roses. The bridal photographer focused on her as he took pictures.

"Your father would pay much money for this," he said, as others in the room including Bimpe giggled.

Chloe wished Mama Joe had been there with her, so she could share the joy she felt. She felt sad that her father never allowed Mama Joe to get involved in decisions about her.

For example, dropping her off with people Chloe knows by the skin of her teeth. Papa Joe had assumed Chloe would meet his expectations that she would be safe, fit in and have fun.

Chloe began to wonder what kind of father he was.
*"Is this his way of showing love to me, or does he trust these people more than her mother?"*, she asked herself. began to realise she could switch from happy beliefs to depressing notions. "Is this good?" she queried herself.

"Chloe, it's time to go to church,"
Bimpe called out, bringing Chloe back from her wandering reflections.

"The bride is ready. Let's go! Let's go. You would like it. Don't worry; I am here. I would help you. I have done a lot of this before."

*"I wish I was the same and as good as you!"*
Chloe ruminated to herself as she walked out of the house with Bimpe. Chloe froze as she watched the dazzling bride. The bride swung around, taking pre-wedding pictures with her family.

She imagined herself someday in a wedding gown eventually, but, *would she ever?* Chloe followed the other flower girls as they walked ahead of the bride. They filled the church with people; there were no spare seats. Some people had to enjoy the wedding service sitting outside the church building, under the scorching sun.

The flower girls scattered flower petals on the floor as they walked in front of the bride. With a boost in her confidence, Chloe carried herself in a classy manner as she walked down the aisle. She soaked up the many benevolent spoken pleasant comments from the surrounding crowd.

Chloe was unaware that her beauty was as fresh as the sunrise. It meant that she soon became the centre of attraction, outshining the bride. Once Chloe dropped the last flower petal in front of the church, they led her to the seat in the front pew.

Chloe began to imagine herself once again, as a bride walking down the aisle with her prince. Like a thunderclap, she remembered her teacher's words:

*"Who would ever marry you?"*

She froze and without a sound, cried inside.

After the wedding service, the excited crowd gathered outside the church. The married couple took pictures with their guests. Chloe saw her father from afar mingling with his friends.

"Father! Father!" Chloe called out, running up to him and holding on to his hands.

Her father was too busy to respond to her. Until Mr Williams, one of his friends acknowledged her presence. (a well-known womaniser going by Mama Joe's description)

"You have a fair one as a daughter, my friend. I wish she had grown up straight away." He fixed his seducing gaze on her.

Chloe looked at him with a puzzled face and a dutiful smile, wondering what he meant by his comments.

"Are you ready to pay the price?" Papa Joe replied without a doubt, with his deep tone.

"I am and would be ready to pay triple the price for one," Mr Williams responded, with a charming smile.

They both laughed, as Papa Joe finally wrapped his arms around Chloe.

Chloe did not understand Mr Williams and her father's conversation. The way Mr Williams fixed his eyes on her body made her feel uncomfortable. She kept quiet but ruminated to herself.

*"Mother will, with assurance know what it means. I'll ask her once I get home."*

Bimpe came to fetch Chloe, and they drove them to the reception and later back to the groom's house. Chloe noticed that Papa Joe was not around to take her back home. It was at about seven pm.

*"Has my daddy finally forgotten I exist?"* pondered Chloe as she started to worry.

She took stock of the situation. Bimpe had been picked up by her mother about thirty minutes ago. She soon realised that she was one of the youngest kids around and felt lonely without Bimpe.

As the night party started, Aunt Banks took Chloe outside, where there was a live band playing loud music. A dancing area stretched out in front of the group.

Chloe sat in the front row to enjoy the music. Before she knew it, her legs were moving to the rhythm. Chloe welcomed the jollof rice and soft drink when it got to her and ate with annoyance.

She had eaten little at the reception and was now starting to feel starved.

About an hour later, the bride and groom danced. They dressed in their glamorous golden native attires. After a while, she noticed everyone around her had gone to the dancing floor.

Chloe caught the energy of the dancing and joined in with the crowd. The crowd 'sprayed' so much money.

A custom that ensured that the couple is distinguished for a beautiful life together. Chloe watched as the Naira notes rained down on the couple. There was a frenzy of activity as guests bagged the money for the dancers.

First, the bride and the groom left the dance floor, slipping away to get ready to go for their honeymoon. Later, the groom's family stopped dancing; there was cleaning up of the stage done.

Chloe continued to dance to the music. She was so caught up in the rhythm that she hadn't noticed that the crowd on the dance floor had reduced. She was enjoying herself so much that she forgot she was dancing.

It was like a 'dance spirit' enveloped her and swung her little body left and right. The rhythm and melody of traditional music matched her steps. She watched the crowd come up the dancing area, 'spraying' her with money. Everyone praised her dancing skills.

The music stopped at midnight for a short while after the married couple left for their honeymoon. The dance floor would open all night for the guests to continue to enjoy themselves.

Once again, Chloe stirred her dancing feet to the music and danced away into the night.

This time around, Mr Williams was with her on the dancing floor spraying her with money. All she could remember was the money; she was not aware of what happened after that.

At about four am, she still found herself on the dance floor. The band had got ready to leave as the night party crowd had thinned out. The dancing exhausted Chloe. As she staggered into the doorway of the house, an adult noticed her. She assisted her to the sofa where she fell fast asleep.

Papa Joe arrived at about seven am to take Chloe home. She woke up feeling sore and sorry for herself as her body responded to the pain that burnt all over. The housemaid helped Chloe collect her belongings from the room. Her father chatted with Mr and Mrs Banks, who recounted how Chloe had taken over the dance floor.

Aunt Banks handed the two bags of money gathered for Chloe to Papa Joe. She felt so embarrassed that she could not recollect the previous night. How had she made a scene that led to them heading home with so much money? *"Was I drugged or something?"* Chloe dug her memory to retrieve answers.

Chloe told Mama Joe about all that had happened from the moment her Dad dropped off. Till the moment Papa Joe came to pick her up, she spared no detail.

To Chloe, it was as if she had been on a time travel adventure and without warning, back to reality. Mama Joe did not say much to all Chloe said, especially about Mr Williams.

Pacing all over the room with excitement, she expressed to Mama Joe about the two bags of money. She discussed with her how she had danced throughout the night. Her mother carried her on her laps and began praying for her.

"Lord, lay your hands on my sweet child for good. Let her know you before she ends up with the wrong company."

Still exhausted, Chloe wondered why her mother did not say much. She became scared of what could happen to her. For now, Chloe was glad she was safely in her mother's arms. Chloe laid her head on her chest and fell asleep.

# ENCOUNTER WITH THE REDEEMER

*Salvation is found in no one else,*
*for there is no other name*
*under heaven is given to mankind*
*by which we must be saved.*

Chloe's years of her distinctive childhood experiences rolled away. It was time for secondary school. Chloe did not gain admission to the secondary school of her choice.

She knew she had difficulty reading, especially pronouncing new words and spelling. Chloe loved arithmetic, albeit there was no support or encouragement to be the best. Something she realised affected her resolve and results. She could not discuss these observations with her overbearing father, or helpless mother.

Chloe reflected on an evening after her eleventh birthday. Papa Joe locked her up in his study, but he never listened to her. As usual, Papa Joe yelled her name from her room.

"Chloe! Chloe, have you finish reading the book I assigned to you for the past two weeks?"
Frightened Chloe rushed out to her underwhelming father flashing the book in front of her.

"Dad, I am sorry, I...I... is not..." the words were yet spoken when she heard a blazing slap on her cheek.

"No, dad, I am..." Once again, he slapped and pushed her into his study.

This time, Chloe starting urinating on herself, in desperation. She remained perturbed with resentment about her relationship with him.

"You would remain in this room until you finish reading this book! You would have to produce a summary of each chapter. I need to ensure you read it."

To make matters worse, her older siblings who could help were now living away from home. Chloe felt very disappointed in herself and her hidden inabilities. Her inadequacies drove her even further into solitude.

She taught her father would use his connections to assist. She made sure he knew which school she would love to attend.

But he refused to speak to anyone on her behalf. He insisted that Chloe join the secondary school the school board allocated her to attend. Even with its bad reputation.

Her relationship with the Saviour was the only reason. The only reason she could give for his increased ill-treatment towards her.

It happened on an Easter morning. Papa Joe sent her off to the church with her sister, because he was not in the mood to attend church. Chloe wore her flowery maxi dress passed down to her from Sarah, her older sister. Mama Joe adjusted the length of the dress to fit her.

Chloe loved the dress, but she struggled with "hand-me-downs" from her older sister. Sarah seemed to have an 'entitlement' to new clothes. She only got new clothes during the festive seasons. A sense of envy flooded her heart.

*"I wish I were born before her,"* she pondered as she tied her headscarf.

"Let's go!" Sarah hurried her out of the house. Stepping out of the gates in silence, Chloe wondered why Sarah was keen to leave home earlier than usual. On the way, they headed to her brother Joe, friend's place of worship.

"I heard they have a lovely youth group," Sarah; said as she blinked her eyelids. She persuaded Chloe to go along with the change of plans.

"I have longed for a visit since the day Joe told us about the church."

Chloe was dragging her feet, unwilling to attend anywhere, apart from Papa's place of worship.

"Do you think we should go?" Sarah continued.

"We are already on our way to Papa's house of worship. I don't want to be in trouble," Chloe replied at once, voicing her discomfort about the idea.

"We won't be in trouble," Sarah assured her.

"We plan to get home as usual, even if we have to leave early." Chloe knew she could not convince Sarah to change her mind. Chloe followed like a sheep led to the slaughter.

The weather was windy. Chloe felt her heart on her lips, tossed to the tune of Sarah's demands. When they arrived, the service had already started.

The steward ushered them to the last few seats at the back of the building. His smile welcomed them with kind-heartedness.

Chloe could not see the preacher, but every word he spoke was like a large hailstone hitting the walls of her heart.

The preacher portrayed the love of a Saviour as that of a father with an everlasting love. His love can fill every void she had felt. He showed that before Chloe was born, He died on a cross as an expression of love for her.

As Chloe listened to the preacher's words; they seemed to flow into her, filling the void. He (the Saviour) was ready to fill her void with love. In tears, she surrendered, walking towards the altar.

Chloe was grateful for this revelation that no man would love her the way He did, laying down His life for her.

The preacher held her small hands and led her in prayer. She felt a warmth and peace she could not describe. After the service, a counsellor led her to a private room. They provided more details about her new relationship.

Unfortunately for Chloe and her sister, events did not go as planned. They arrived home an hour later than the usual time. They had forgotten about Papa Joe in their excitement.

They sang and danced together, holding hands until they got to the front of the gate.

"Oh, dear," exclaimed Chloe. "Papa! We are in trouble, Sarah! He had locked the gates."

Tears started rolling down her eyes.

Sarah dreading the consequences, hugged her as she reminded her not to let go of her new experience. They agreed to remain bold to face the outcome. Banging on the gates brought Papa Joe out of the house. They could see how angry he was as he headed to the portal. Mama Joe ran out right behind him to plead on their behalf, but he ignored her.

"Go back to where you are coming from now! The leader told me you were not at the place of worship. Do you have an explanation for your actions?" shouted Papa Joe waving his belt.

"Pa… Papa, w we wen went toooooo Jo Joeeee's …," Sarah said, trembling in fear. Before she could finish her statement, he opened the gates. He used the belt on them as they escaped into the house crying.

"Did I send you to Joe's church? Do you want to lose your mind like him? I don't want to see you there again."

"Mama! Mama! My body hurts. Papa hurt me. Why does he hate me so much?" Chloe ran into Mama Joe's arms, weeping non-stop.

"He doesn't. You must know he doesn't. Even if he does, you must love him instead of hate. Love is greater than hate,"

Mama replied, rocking Chloe in her arms. Chloe carried mama's words in her heart as she began her new relationship.

After the incident, it was not too long before she realised; she was not the same as the old Chloe any more. She saw herself through the mirror of His words. The Saviour replaced the shame and timidity, she felt, with love.

In the Rescuer's words, **"I have loved you with an everlasting love, before I conceived you,"** touched her heart. Her shame had disappeared, although she was still introverted. When she was with her friends, she was a funny and good company.

Chloe knew He had forgiven her past. The power of His blood washed away that incident with John. She also knew the creator had made her without a glitch; it did not matter if she was not perfect now.

The Saviour filled her with unspeakable joy; her new expression was indescribable.

Chloe's new relationship was heart-warming. A sincere acknowledgement of the debt she could not repay. Her redeemer paid a debt He did not owe, with blood dripping from His sides and with his last breath.

The liberator declared He finished the salvation plan. Creating a fulfilment for Chloe's deep longing, replacing all the guilt she felt. New birth led to new songs. As her love for the Saviour increased, so praises from within her.

Papa Joe soon noticed Chloe's changed life. The realisation that she had met with the emancipator was an abomination to him. He tried all he could to turn her away from the road she had followed.

Papa Joe stopped her from going to the house of worship. He punished her for any little transgression and tried to control her.

Without Papa Joe's knowledge, Chloe grew in faith. She received support and encouragement from her mother, the church, and her siblings. She chose the narrow path, digging a massive wedge between her father and herself.

Papa Joe made decisions that would make her life unbearable. Rather than supporting her and looking out for her best interest.

Her experience in secondary school was the same, despite the joy of her relationship with her Emmanuel. Her classmates were not any better than in primary school.

Chloe found she could not step out of her comfort zone to trust others. Then again, her experience with her teachers was different. Chloe was a favourite with many of her teachers.

She was one of two junior students to head the school literary group. A milestone that created a source of delight to Chloe's shaken world of schooling. The more she felt the teachers liked her, the more her classmates seemed to hate her. Their attitude created a new sense of isolation, but she was happy within.

Chloe had become used to people calling her names. But, she didn't resent the impact the same way she did in primary school. She had found a way of turning their teasing into jokes.

Chloe learnt to tell herself that the new relationship is all that's needed to be complete. She longed for the days when she would make genuine friends with her father and the people; she came across daily. With her heavenly Father, a true friend, she never felt out of place.

Chloe's educational attainment became impeded after the first three years. Because of the poorly rated school and a shortage of good teachers.

As a result, Papa Joe finally moved Chloe from her current school to an all-girls boarding school. He aimed for her to complete her senior secondary school away from the distraction of the church.

Papa Joe had perchance despised the newfound faith she professed. He could have intended the move to knock the belief out of her system. Little did Chloe's father know it was working out to her advantage. The decision drew her closer to the newfound lover she met three years earlier.

The feelings were inexplicable. Chloe could chat with Him, seek Him, praise Him without shame. Only one thing was missing. She never invited her lover to deal with the hidden pains.

The deep depressions of her childhood and inferiority complex she wouldn't face. It seemed gone! Was it forgotten and not dealt with permanently?

In her new school, she did not have to deal with the opposite sex. The boarding school was a perfect place for her to avoid boys' issues altogether.

Chloe only talked with the opposite sex at church or home during school breaks. She listened to her schoolmates discuss their interactions with their boyfriends. A few of the girls, even as teenagers were regular night party lovers off-campus.

That idea never entered her mind because she feared that she was not ready or able to deal with it. Chloe did not attempt to train her mind to conquer her emotions. She often asked herself if this could work against her in the negative?

# EARLY DAYS

*And I... I'm desperate for you*
*And I... I'm lost without you*
Michael W Smith

An evening during study time, Chloe felt a sharp pain around her abdomen. She rushed to the toilet and urinating was right; so painful. She started feeling a burning sensation in her vagina, which compounded her sudden nightmare. The smell of the discharge was awful. Chloe flashed back through the history files in her memory.

"Could this have anything to do with what I did with John when I was barely six-years-old?"

She was so afraid of telling any of her friends about the pain. It wasn't long before her dorm-mate asked her about her constant discomfort. Three days after her pain started, Chloe was looking pale and tired, so the matron called her to her quarters.

It took her breath away to see Papa Joe, sitting opposite the matron with a very downcast face. She faced his usual disposition when she entered the room. It was his, 'You are in trouble' face.

The matron, clearing her throat with a chewing stick between her teeth said, "Come in. I got a report that you have been reacting funny, and the girls are not comfortable. I called your father. He would take you home. Once we get to the bottom of the observed concerns, you can return."

She's horror-struck and embarrassed to find out the matron knew. Chloe suspected one of her dorm-mates had reported her. Papa Joe rose from the seat, thanked the matron and walked out without saying a word.

"Ma," Chloe replied the matron, "Can I take some of my belongings home?"

"No!" said matron, interrupting with a somewhat angry tone.

"Your father is waiting for you outside. Go, go, go join your father! I always thought you were one of the few good ones. I am disappointed!"

Chloe joined Papa Joe and the driver in the car. She was about to get into the back seat, with Papa Joe when he spoke in a bit for the first time.

"Ehn... sit in the passenger seat with the driver. Stupid girl!" He turned to the driver and instructed him, "Take me to the University Hospital."

Chloe had never been this confused in her life.

*"I am sixteen. I love the Saviour. I have not been close to the opposite sex. Even though I see my mates in the*

*hostel, sneaking out at night to have fun. Saviour, I know you forgave me for my past sins. Do I have to still pay for them?"* Still, in pain, Chloe cried with tears flooding her adoring eyes. *"Saviour, please, I plead with you take this pain away. Bring healing please…"*

The driver distracted her from her reflections by his soft touch, covering his hands over hers.

"Small madam, you would be fine," the driver said with his lovely reassuring smile.

The nurses exchanged greetings with Papa Joe and led them to the waiting room. A few minutes later, Chief Gynaecologist walked into the room. After exchanging pleasantries, Chloe eavesdropping heard Papa Joe saying to the doctor.

"The matron called me to her school to discuss her symptoms. She suspects teenage pregnancy."

The doctor replied, "I would deal with Chloe as soon as possible. But I would not suspect pregnancy immediately. I would run all the tests. I have a patient in the office, so one nurse would take care of her."

Papa Joe, with pleasure, replied, "Try to make it as discreet as possible. I would leave Chloe in your care. My driver would be back to pick her. I would call later to discuss the results."

Chloe was to the highest degree, disappointed in her father.

*"How could he believe I would get pregnant? Does Papa Joe not trust me? Is that why he called me stupid and refused to say a word to me? I supposed Mama Joe trained me well? I am not surprised as a Papa Joe thinketh, so he is."*

After Papa Joe left, the nurse took Chloe for the pregnancy test, which was negative. On his return, the gynaecologist did a physical examination of the sore areas. After several tests, he concluded it was 'vaginitis', a toilet infection.

"Spot on! A toilet infection," Chloe reflected.
Owning up, she was happy, tears of sorrow streamed down her cheeks. Chloe could not help feeling hurt by Papa Joe's distrust of her.

At home, it upset Mama Joe when she discovered the day's event. She asked the driver to take Chloe back to school, encouraging her to forgive Papa Joe.

Chloe returned to school with a renewed distrust towards her mates.

"Who would have told a tale behind her?"

The memories of her primary school experiences plagued her again. This time she could take it to the saviour. She found comfort in a relationship with day students and the students' fellowship.

Two of the girls from the school fellowship, particularly interested Chloe, and they soon became friends. One of them was from a wealthy family. But she met the Saviour through the influence of some of her friends.

Unlike Chloe, she was timid and kept her faith a secret from her father. She found the joy of serving the saviour through school communion.

The other girl was Simi; she was from a Muslim home but met the saviour through a different circumstance. As a girl from a Muslim household, she lived with the experience of polygamy. They all had with their fathers' painful experiences.

Their familiarities bonded their friendship throughout school and beyond. For the first time, Chloe knew that association with girls was not a bad idea. It only depends on the girl and the things that bind you together.

In the three girls – it was the family, Saviour and the desire to make something out of their lives.

As a strict faith school, its expected students to attend all masses. It was all about the life she lived before her encounter with the saviour. She would never be carried away by the activities. She felt all the zealous one would come to know the saviour as she did.

On the one hand, it was comforting they had some faith, and the other side it seems like zeal without knowledge. Two situations bothered her in the boarding house.

First, some of these faith students were always around the male leader, in the pastorage. Could anything be happening to these girls beyond the eyes, than she could perceive?

Her mind often flashed back, to an incident that occurred to her when she was about 10 years old.

Papa Joe had taken Sarah and herself to the early morning service. He had to wait behind for one of the harvest committee meetings. Meaning the girls had to occupy themselves until the session ended. Sarah wandered off with some of her friends.

Chloe, as usual, was left alone to wander around by herself. Chloe loved flowers and thus followed the trails of flowers leading to the pastorage.

All of a sudden, she felt a touch on her shoulder. Lily-livered, Chloe looked back to see one of the student priests standing behind her. She attempted to run. But he wrapped his hands around her waist, which tampered down any attempt to run or scream.

Chloe knew she was in the church environment. In theory, it was safe to let down her guard. Make a clean breast, Chloe was still trembling within. She minimised any contact with the massive figure in front of her.

He questioned her with a low-pitched accent. "Pretty girl, what is your name, and what are you doing here?"
In fear, Chloe replied,

"My name is Lola, and I want to wee, please, where is the toilet?"

She knew she was lying, but she would not reverse her name. She would, in words of one syllable play along.

The handsome looking priest put his hands around her shoulder and said, "Let me take you there."

With discomfort, she felt his hands drew her tiny body closer to him. He led her to one of the toilets in the pastorage.

She was amazed to see a lot of young ladies around. Some were heading in and out of their private rooms. Chloe wondered what they were all doing there. When she came out of the toilet, the young priest was still standing aloft awaiting her return.

This time he said, "Do you feel better now?"

"Yes, thank you. I am very grateful."

"Where are your parents? Or better still, who did you come to church with?"

"My dad, he is attending the harvest committee meeting."

"Do you know how long he would be at the meeting?"

"Not sure, but he said we could play around, I sense I should go. The meeting may have ended."

This time, the priest asked her to wait to find out from another person if the meeting was over. Chloe felt he was caring to find out about her father and had a genuine interest in her. In the depth of her being, the image of John brought an awful feeling.

It affected her exchange of words with this priest. Is he going to do the same thing John did? Do I need to run? Do all these girls know what would happen to them if these men are like John? The touch of the priest's hand on her shoulder interrupted her deep thoughts.

"Okay, Lola, the meeting is still going on."

"Thank you, but can I go now," she asked in a ladylike manner, looking away from him.

"Are you always this shy? Do you know you are so beautiful, as the rising sun? I have seen no little girl this beautiful. How old are you?"

"I am ten, and yes, I am shy." Nodding her head.

"Do you want to tell me what happened to your teeth, it makes you so unique."

Chloe looked away and declined chivalrously. "Alright, do you want to see my room?"

"His room? Why? For what?" panic mused racing through her mind. Chloe turned to run away, but he stretched out his hands to hold her back.

"I don't bite, and my room doesn't swallow. Come in and take a cup of juice."

His priestly robe wrapped around her body, leading her further into the world of the unknown.

Chloe froze within, looking forward to the worst outcome. The priest led her into his room. To her amazement, the room was more colourful than she can imagine.

There were posters of celebrities on the wall. Chloe questioned the lifestyles outside the duties of the priest. He led her to sit on the chair, pulling it straight to face him as she sat on his bed.

"Oh, I forgot, the juice."

He stood up to pick a cup from his small cupboard and opened his fridge to bring out the cartoon of '5 Alive' orange juice.

Chloe tore and panicked with several in-between thoughts.

*"Where in the world is Sarah? How can she not think of me? Mama Joe, why does she not attend this church? I would have been safe with her. What if I take this juice and something happens to me?"*

"If I take this juice, can I go? I need to find my sister. "

"Lola, do you have a sister as beautiful as you too."

*"Did the priest a moment ago rub his hands on my lap?"* She panicked, and the cup shook, spilling some juice on her cloth. The priest got back to reality at once.

"Yes, of course. How old is your sister?"

"She is 15 years old, would be 16 soon, she went off with her friends." Chloe drank the juice in her cup in a flash. She moved the chair away from the direction of the priest, who did not oppose any of her actions.

Chloe stood up, dropped the cup on the table with her hand shaking and reached out for the doors. She turned the doorknob. Lo-and-behold! It's locked.

Chloe looked back with tears rolling down her face.

"Please, let me go, please. I want to look for my sister. I would come back with her if you permit me. I would come here whenever I come to church, and please let me go. Please! Please."

Chloe slid down the back of the door sobbing.

"I am in another deep trouble. How did I get here?" Chloe screamed within.

The priest walked towards her and carried her up. He wrapped his hands around her and said,

"It's okay darling; I would not hurt you. Lola dear, you have to be comfortable with me before we become close friends. I would let you go now."

"Thank you," Chloe muttered under her breath.

The tears from her face soaked into the priestly robe.

"If you want to bring your sister, I would love to be friends with both of you. "

"Yes, sure I will," drawing away from his embrace. Chloe said all he wanted to hear.

Once the door becomes opened, her goal was to be out of his room in a flash.

Offering her his white handkerchief, he said, "Lola, clean your face, we don't want anyone to see your beautiful tears. Do we?"

"No, not at all priest."

He offered to help refresh her face, and he unlocked his door. Chloe walked out as someone let out of the lion's den without any scratch.

"Oh Daniel, is this how you felt when you came out? We learnt about you in Sunday school today."

Chloe walked post-haste away in distraught, looking for Sarah in fear. Once out of the pastorage, she ran toward Papa Joe's car.

She was confronted by her angry father, who was annoyed that Chloe wasted his time.

She wandered into the unknown and blamed herself for it. Within Chloe's mind, this girl knew; there was a hidden world. Chloe was only glad she was safe once more.

Chloe, in reality, hoped there was no other priest like the one in her past in the school pastorage.

Chloe's second concern was the level of dysfunctionality displayed by some of her mates. It defined her senior years with tales of girls sneaking out of the boarding house.

Rumours had it that the parties between the girls and another boys' only school were a regular occurrence. The girls had to bribe the gateman. He would let them out of the compound without the knowledge of the strict matron. Before dawn, they would return to share stories of their parties.

A good description of the group of girls was the 'posh bred.' They would often spend their holidays out of the country. They had the latest gadgets and could afford anything. She prayed they would meet and love the saviour as she did.

On the other hand, Chloe had less than what she needed, but she learnt to be content with the little she got from Mama Joe. To hurt her more, Papa Joe had refused to support her in the boarding house.

Great family friends from the church helped her. They would often provide all the provisions and other necessary feminine needs.

On occasions, when Mama Joe or Sarah would visit all her mates would look forward to the food. Most times, Chloe might end up at a loss of her food, because everyone wanted to have a taste of Mama Joe's precious dishes.

Living with her faith and loving her saviour was hard. Sometimes she felt tempted to enjoy living like the surrounding girls. It was a constant war with her.

To worsen her inner pressure to conform, her roommates often masturbate. It was a strange concept to Chloe. She would imagine the sequelae they derived from the experience, remembering 'Ikebe super.'

After watching her roommates and a few other girls, Chloe fought the battle within to give it a go. The girls described it as enjoying a self-made pleasure.

"You don't have to get it from the boys, as our friends in the other rooms do."

"How does this make you feel?" She asked.

"It's satisfactory. Have you not watched porn before?" another asked.

"Chloe is a saint! Do saint watch porn?" Shout out the next.

"Even if she has not watched one, she can experience this too," another responded laughing.

"The saint is waiting for her prince charming to handle her with tender loving-kindness."
Another said as they all laughed at Chloe simplicity on the topic.

Chloe felt disappointed and embarrassed. She carried her books and left for the study room. The images and the actions of the girls bothered her for weeks.

She fought the notions of giving pleasure to herself, like the pictures she viewed as a child. She knew it would be wrong to have a premarital experience with the opposite sex.

*"But is there anywhere in His words, that prohibit me to give pleasure to myself?"*

Chloe would question herself each time, fighting the temptation to succumb.

✿ ✿ ✿

One evening, Chloe went into the toilet. She attempted to try out what she had drawn her mind to cultivate.

The negative force raging within her overcame her. She sat on the bathroom and did the same thing as the girls do in the room.

At first, she felt nothing, but all of a sudden, she felt a force propelled her to the next level. Then the climax and then in tears, she cried, "What have I done?"

She felt the same excitement the girls spoke about in the room. But it doesn't end there; she believed she lost something. She lost her peace. Laying on her bed at bedtime, she tried talking to the saviour. He seemed a far way, a far distance away.

The next few days, she repeated the self-pleasure she craved for with every passing thought. It was addictive like a class A drug.

The more she did, the less she experienced the presence and sweet communion with her saviour. Chloe started losing interest in her friends and attended less of the meeting.

Simi was the first to notice her displeasure in their company.

She exchanged company with new friends, her roommates. They became confused about her new disposition towards them. The more, the merrier, they felt moving her further away from her first love.

Simi called her for a friendly meeting in one of the classes. Chloe did not show up, knowing what the meeting was all about. But, her two friends went over to her room all the same. After exchanging pleasantries, they got down to business.

"Chloe, you know we love you. You know whatever you are going through, we are here to support you," Simi started.

"I know, and I agreed. Nothing is wrong with me," Chloe snapped.

"Okay, can we study together? Wc wanted to spend the evening with you."

"Wait! Don't you have homes to go? Simi, your father would kill you if you are out after six pm," Chloe protested, wanting them to leave her alone. She was not ready to uncover the deep shame she felt. Or disclose the desire to carry out graphic actions on herself.

*"How do I explain what I am doing to anyone? With confidence, they would condemn me. It's obvious! Deliverance! They would prescribe deliverance. They would not make any effort to understand."*

Her reflections were interrupted by Simi.

"Chl! Let's go, both our mummies are covering for us."

"Did you discuss me with your mums?" Chloe spoke in shock, sitting up on her bed.

"Yes, of course. We miss your company, and you have withdrawn from us these few weeks. We needed to get closer, or we lose you completely."

"It doesn't matter what happened, and we want you. You don't have to tell us. You know the Redeemer knows, and he understands." Simi continued to speak.

"Remember, we share that He loves us. Despite what we do in the past, today and the future."

Simi's words hit Chloe's heart like a sandstorm in the desert. She needed to sort out this wrong path she had followed herself. She needs to find her way back to the Saviour.

The rest of the evening they spent together, sharing all the lost times, laughing and eating snacks. Chloe, however, was beating herself up with guilts, unknown to her friends. The girls left at about seven pm. Another hour later than planned. They prayed together, hoping they don't get in trouble with their fathers.

Chloe felt loved, for the first time after a few weeks. The girls' encouragement did not bring all the peace she lost. It was time to talk to the Saviour.

"I am sorry," Chloe called out in tears on her lower bunk bed facing the wall.

She called out in pain for the path she had followed, distracted by the fellowship with her roommates.

Before Chloe slept off, she heard the still small voice speaking to her heart.

"My Child, don't you know your body is my temple?"

"I know, I am sorry," Chloe said in response.

**"Offer your body, soul and spirit to me as an acceptable offering. I loved you enough to give it all for you. I want you to give me every part of you, even the sacred parts of you. Remember, there is a time for everything. At that right time, you can express it to me in pleasure. For now, walk with me in purity."**

Peace like a river flooded her heart; He forgave her. Lesson learnt, my child if sinners convince you to follow them, do not walk the path of sorrows with them.

# EMOTIONAL AWARENESS

*Every love we feel –*
*Our love for partners, our children,*
*our friends, and our community*
*– comes with its own set of complications.*
Alexandra Stoddard

Few months after her experience with Papa's distrust, some new neighbours had moved into the building opposite Chloe's. She rushed into the house from school with excitement dragging her backpack with her.

"Mama! Mama, we're got, neighbours!" Mama Joe stepped out of the kitchen, cleaning her hands with a napkin.

"My love, you are back! At least, greet me before the neighbour's news. Would you like to join me in the kitchen?" Chloe knelt before her mother as she hugged her waist, laughing.

"Sorry mama, the neighbour's clothes, spread outside carried me away," Chloe said as she rose to give her mother a peck. Mama Joe led her into the kitchen.

To her surprise, Mama had visitors having lunch with her. The visitors sat on the old dinner table used by her family alone. Visitors were entertained usually in the dining room.

Chloe's countenance changed to her shy disposition. In the presence of two handsome young men, a young girl and presumably their mother.

*"These boys look good!"* she echoed to herself. Chloe glimpsed at them without being noticed.

*"The girl looks like a snob; the woman is classy; where is their dad?"*

Mama Joe interrupted her musing conclusions, when she said, "Chloe, meet Ryan, Nathaniel and Sandra. They all attend the university's secondary school. Caroline is their mum. They moved into the neighbourhood six weeks ago." She continued.

"Caroline, Ryan, Nathaniel and Sandra, meet my last-child, Chloe. She arrived from the boarding school a moment ago for the break."

Chloe went toward Caroline, knelt and greeted her. "Welcome, ma. Hope you have settled into the neighbourhood."

"Thank you, my dear," Caroline replied. Caroline added, "Mama Joe, your daughter is well-mannered."

Chloe replied, "Thank you, ma." To the rest, she said "Hi."

One of the two boys smote her imaginations. Chloe added,

"I would catch up with you guys. I want to change into something comfortable."

Chloe hurried out of the kitchen before they could reply to her greetings. Using her hands to redress herself, "Saviour, please, I plead with you take these odd feelings away. They are boys! Please…"

Mama Joe said to the visitors as she stepped out. "She is the shy one, the baby of the house. Don't worry. When you get to know her, she is a sweet girl."

The children replied to Mama Joe, together with "Yes, ma."

✿ ✿ ✿

"Mama! Mama!" Chloe called out, running down the staircase once the visitors were out of sight.

"Mama, you didn't warn me we had visitors."

Mama Joe replied, smiling,

"Chloe, dear, you came in with your big announcement. I couldn't inform you. Sorry, love."

"Mama; tell me about them. I want to hear everything. Are they nice? Weird? And so on. You know, we've not had neighbours for a while."

Eager Chloe said as she pushed her mother's hands with her dimpled face, shouting for all the gist.

"Take it easy," Mama persuaded Chloe to slow down. "I have little to say. It surprised me they visited."

Chloe replied, "For real?"

Mama Joe picking up her bag to go out continued,

"Since they moved in about a month ago, I have not spoken to them. They kept to themselves."

"Oh!" Chloe added as she reclined on the sofa.

"It could be when you interact with them, you might change things around here. Why did you hurry out of the

kitchen? Are you boys shy now? I saw you with ruminative eyes examining each one of them."
Mama Joe teased her.

Chloe changed the topic to end the discussion right away.

"Mama, where is Sarah?"

"She has gone back to university. I am heading for the market; I made your favourite meal. Eat and rest," Mama replied as she stepped out.

Chloe tried to avoid the neighbour's two sons. She kept a low-profile friendship with their sister, Sandra.

*"Sandra differs from my first impression. She is fun and friendly,"* Chloe believed.

She watched as new relationships blossomed between the neighbours.

"I have never been confronted with such good-looking guys. It made her question the feelings arousing within her."

She took extra care of her appearance.

*"This is kind of weird!"* she exclaimed to herself.

Anytime she came across the boys, especially Ryan, Chloe would ask herself.

*"How do I intend to keep the deal I made to myself to keep men at arm's length?"*

It was difficult to control her thoughts.

*"I have a crush! What do I do? Mama Joe has already teased me about them. It would not be a good idea to bring it up."*

In the following months, she loosened up in stages. She made friends with Nathaniel, the neighbour's second son.

Nathaniel was a light-hearted young teenager; his smiles could crack the hardest soul. Chloe loved the way he dressed in an orderly way, usually with his white shirt.

*"Funny how some boys get attached to a single colour,"* Chloe cogitated.

She smiled at him on her way from running an errand for Mama Joe. He was a homely lad who enjoyed spending time in the kitchen, an unusual trait for a teenage boy.

She soon became fond of Nathaniel because they shared a love for cooking. Often, they discussed the next meal they would prepare and exchanged cooking tips.

Apart from cooking, Chloe's other hobbies were gardening and fishing. She also kept a small snail farm. Nathaniel enjoyed spending time with her at the river fishing. They roasted them afterwards.

He disliked snails and the slime residue it leaves behind. Chloe enjoyed every opportunity to 'pull his leg' and scare Nathaniel with her snails. Nathaniel, who was competitive, loved to compete on who would catch the first fish.

The loser of the contest would usually have to go home wet and start the fire for roasting the fish. Others wouldn't join them for the hard work. They, however, enjoyed eating the fish with garri (roasted cassava flakes) while cracking jokes.

Ryan, Nathaniel's older brother, was a nerd and seemed to be his mother's favourite. From Chloe's viewpoint, she treated him differently from Nathaniel. Friends from the neighbourhood would gather to discuss.

Usually, in the evenings, play, and crack jokes about school. Chloe avoided discussions with Ryan because she felt he was the high-minded one. Despite this, she liked Ryan affectionately from Nathaniel. Ryan didn't seem to notice her. She wondered why she was becoming attracted to the boy.

Chloe felt everything within her did not want to think of a young man. She learnt every day to ignore the pressing temptation. To give her feelings away whenever she was around Ryan.

One Saturday evening, Nathaniel and Chloe went on their regular fishing expedition. Nathaniel was usually over-dressed in his white polo shirt and black jeans. Chloe, on the other hand, wore one of her old dresses suitable for fishing and surprises. They enjoyed themselves.

Out of the blue, the clouds gathered faster than they could have imagined. It started raining before they could pack up to leave. Nathaniel panicked by the edge of the water and fell into the river.

He had not experienced fishing in bad weather. The sudden splash and the noise in the river made Chloe turn around in sharp contrast. She saw Nathaniel panicking in the water.

"Chloe, help! Help!" Nath screamed.
She had never seen him so afraid since she met him. Acknowledging in the panic of his yelling herself, Chloe jumped into the river as Nathaniel yelled for help.

She caught him by the hand and said, "I've got you. Hold on to my arms."

She dragged him to the edge of the water, with all the strength she had.

"Glad to be out!" He exclaimed, sitting on the bank of the river.

Nathaniel held on very much to Chloe, whispering, "Thank you! Thank you!"
Both were from tip to toe soaked, as the rain fell with poise on them.

Nath was the first person who would thank her for her kindness, in a profound way, apart from her family. He did it in such an affectionate manner.

Chloe responded aloof as she let go in a tad. With such a swift dynamism, she walked over to the bag and packed up to leave. Nathaniel walked over behind her, saying in a melancholic tone.

"Chloe, did I do something or say something wrong?"

His voice was like a little child seeking approval from his mother. He reached out to hold her hands in the rain.

Chloe replied with embarrassment. She hid the breeze of affection; they both experienced a moment ago.

"No, not at all. We need to head home; cos your mummy would be worried sick that her baby boy is not around."

"Hey Chloe, I am not a baby, what gives you that impression?"

Chloe said this because she reasoned if something had happened to Nathaniel. His mother would blame her for it.

*"Even though I am glad he thanked me, I couldn't bear it if something had happened. Wouldn't want to put us into more trouble than we are already in."*

Nathaniel interrupted Chloe's imaginations as he continued. "Can we talk about your sudden change in the mood?"

She was feeling embarrassed in her wet clothes and replied, "Mood change? Not at all. Nath, don't we talk? We talk every day about everything. We talk, right! What else do you perhaps want to talk about?"

She avoided eye contact, turning her gaze away from him. She knew Nath's attracted to her, and that she did not have the same feeling. Instead, her appeal was to his brother, Ryan.

The sudden reality of his attraction shook her. She was not sure how to handle it other than to defend herself by the sudden outburst.

Nathaniel surprised but infectiously smiling as he said,

"It's okay. When you feel comfortable talking about it, I am always here."

They walked back home in the rain in a world of silence.

*"Poor Nath, how I wish I could be more honest with you, Lord forgive me,"* she reflected.

*"Is this the beginning of the end of an innocent friendship?"* Chloe pondered as they walked along.

Chloe could not sleep all night as she tossed from side to side. She wondered whether she was heading for the trouble she wouldn't be able to handle.

*"All I wanted is a friend. Why did Nath hold my hands that way? Can you imagine the way he fixed his eyes on me? Is Nath trying to communicate something else? Is that the way a boy looks into a girl's eyes when he falls in love?*

*I very much think I shouldn't give Nath any funny ideas any more. What will I do with Ryan? Even though I like him, he seems not to swoop on me the way as Nath did this evening. Why does he not even look my way?"*

As these notions played in her mind all night, she remembered the Saviour's words.

**"Do not awake your emotions when it is not ripe for it."**

Her Saviour and Mama Joe were right again. She talked with Him for a while and then drifted off to sleep.

Chloe avoided Nath's company over the next few days. She found reasons to be busy indoors while the rest of the neighbours spent time together.

A week later, there was a knock on the door. Nath stood helpless at the doorway and said,

"I missed fishing. Can we spend time together?"
As she opened her mouth to say, "No," Mama Joe spoke from behind.

"I reason that, you children have little to do around here. I am waiting to eat roasted fish tonight. Head out!"

To Chloe, that was the most boring time she had spent with Nath. She could not pretend that the last time never happened.

*"Did Mama notice anything wrong with us? She is too smart. Was she trying to matchmake us or something?"* Chloe pondered in her mind like a broken record player.

Several times, Nath tried to break the ice to get through to her, but she was somewhat too scared.

She pored over the rhythm of the flowing river for answers to her plaguing thoughts.

Getting home, Mama Joe had already made a fire for the fish. Because of the unexplainable silence between the friends, Nath made an excuse.

"I have to hurry home to make dinner."
The best he could come up with to avoid being in Chloe's company for longer. Chloe missed her friend but did not know how to express herself.

"I am so lame at handling a friendship!" She criticised herself.

Chloe walked over to the fence from where she watched Nath as he climbed the stairs. She kept talking to his sister as a distraction. Nath's mother reached out from the front door and invited her for dinner. She accepted, adding,

"I would bring some fish along." She informed Mama Joe and went across to Nath's house.

All Chloe noticed was Ryan's unwelcoming face staring at her. She was glad the evening was uneventful. Chloe wondered what to do with Ryan and her feelings as she walked home in the dark.

# FIRST CRUSH

*Many claims to have unfailing love,*
*but a faithful person who can find?*

A month after the dinner in Nath's house, she was ready to resume school. She was glad she could interact with Nath, with no reference to the 'rainy day.'

Nathaniel seemed to have gotten her message. Lately, if Nath said "Hi," Chloe would reply with "Hi."

Things were awkward, and she didn't know how to deal with him. Sometimes she wished she had allowed him to speak. It is possible that what he intended to say had nothing to do with an emotional attraction to her.

Chloe decided not to tell Mama Joe about him; she had already teased about the boys' effect.

Chloe was able to cover up her feelings for Ryan and Nath's distractions. She returned light-hearted to school after the holidays.

Each time she had a call or a visit from home, she was quick to find out how her neighbours were doing. Her sister provided all the information about them. She was not courageous enough to let out the secret notions in her heart.

Often during evening study periods, the senior students and her mates' gist. Their discussions filled with their adventures with their boyfriends or the famous prohibited night parties.

Chloe would allow her ideas to drift away from schoolwork to Nath and Ryan. She would write poems to express her feelings and ease the pressure of the conflict in her mind. One of her poems was;

> *I can't fathom it*
> *With a thought of you in my heart*
> *When I close my eyes,*
> *I think of you first, like the rising of the sun.*
> *When I open my eyes,*
> *Smiles rush to my lips, like streams of waters*
> *Just at the thought of you.*
> *Thinking of you*
> *Makes me want to have every minute of you.*
> *I longed for the day I cannot*
> *Do without you*
> *Just thinking of you*
> *Makes my day*
> *I wish I could express it.*
> *Just the way I feel*
> *That I can't do without you.*

Chloe often felt out of place in the company of others. Chloe knew it was out of place to focus on the imaginations flooding her mind. Chloe sought the purity of her philosophy as her greatest desire. Those around her partly influenced this pattern.

The Saviour was never too far from her, putting a check on her reflections. He directed her to focus on the needs of others through her pastoral care. With time, the previous thought patterns faded away at a snail's pace.

A few weeks into the new session, there was an inter-school debate. The contest between Chloe's and Ryan's schools was at Chloe's school. It was an excellent opportunity for her to see her 'first-time crush' after six weeks from home.

The girls let out a noise as the college bus drove in. The debate team hopped off the bus, confident as expected.

She saw Ryan. He looked handsome in his checked shirt, dark blue fitted uniform. He had on a sunglass to hide his eyes from the reflections of the sun.

The moment Chloe saw him smiling with his friend, her eyes sparkled. Her heart started to skip in beats like a horse galloping over the hills.

The Head girl tapped her shoulder, jolting her out of her dreamy world.

"Chloe, we need your presence in the hall to get the girls settled. Why are you looking like you saw a ghost?"

"Nothing!" Pretending nothing happened.

The full school hall was now louder because the "boys" were around. The girls were more interested in boys than the debate competition itself.

Chloe knew her school's debate team were good but was not sure whether they could win against Ryan's.

Chloe was the assistant assembly prefect, whose role was to maintain order at any school gathering. She walked onto the stage with the Assembly and Pastoral Care Prefect.

The big hall went quiet as they stood in front of the assembly with their brown and white pinafore uniform. They wore half knee socks. She was representing the standard of the dress required for the whole school. Chloe and Ryan made eye contact immediately.

Ryan was seated in one of the designated seats at the front of the hall. She raised her fingers a little to say hi to him. Ryan smiled back with the same finger gesture. It delighted her to receive a sweet acknowledgement of her presence for the first time.

*"How I wish he does the same at home,"* she pondered, trying to concentrate on the task ahead.

She read the announcements and returned to her seat. Being the pastoral care captain, Chloe sat in the front row. It gave her a good view of Ryan. She informed some of her friends that one of the boys was her neighbour.

Soon enough, the teasing started,

"Finally! Chloe has a boyfriend." Chloe already used to tease; she took it in a cavalier fashion.

Smiling to herself, she reflected, *"Only if all wishes could be true!"*

Ryan was wearing his school uniform, although he looked much older. A good-looking, muscular young lad with his overbearing Afro haircut. Though the cooling fans were at the highest level, she watched him every so often use his handkerchief to wipe his eyebrows.

His big brown eyes were the very features that attracted her to him. She watched as Ryan with vigour rounded up as the last speaker. After the debate, Ryan's school emerged as winners.

Chloe felt so proud of him. All the girls in the school were so excited for the boys. It was unusual to have boys around as a single-gender school.

She felt so delighted as she pushed through the crowd to give     Ryan and the rest of his team hugs of congratulations.

Still, she didn't dare to express any hint of her feelings. She walked the team to their school bus.

Ryan and Chloe talked about home and all the other neighbourhood gist. Once boarded, she waved 'goodbye', hoping to catch up with him at the end of the school term.

The next opportunity Chloe had, she called Mama Joe to narrate the event of the day. All of a sudden, she noticed the phone line was silent.

"Mama, are you there?" Chloe asked to reaffirm she was having a conversation.

Mama Joe responded, "Child, I am here. You sound more than usually enthusiastic about discussing an event. Chloe, you were not representing the school. Neutral thinking! Is it because your neighbour was part of the team? Am I sensing something rather different in the tone of your voice?"

Chloe knew it would be a lie if she responded with a 'No.'

She was not sure she should express her feelings for Ryan to Mama now. *"What if she treats me like Papa Joe did during the pregnancy scare episode?"*

Chloe replied, "Mama, you know what? My call credit is running out. I would call you later." Without delay, she ended the call.

"At least, this is true," she told herself as she hung up the phone.

After a rigorous academic and challenging term, the school was finally over. Chloe had made sure that she never referred to Ryan and Nathaniel. Even when Mama Joe mentions them during her communications, she reframed from speaking about them.

Chloe returned home to discover that her neighbours had vacated the building. Mama Joe told her they had travelled abroad, to continue their studies a few days earlier.

As already established, Ryan's mother was too secretive. But, that she would drop a 'bombshell' of their sudden travel! An unexpected turn of events for Chloe.

The secret crush for Ryan faded slowly but surely within Chloe's heart! She felt Ryan would never have noticed her because she did not seem to be good enough for him. In conclusion, her primary school teacher could be right; Who would care to admire her?

The shame she carried from the past soon eroded her reflection s and feelings. She laid on her bed in the night with a ray of moonlight floating in.

She remembered every moment she spent with them. Most notably, her first experience of a pure friendship with the opposite sex, Nathaniel.

Chloe started to prepare for university after she completed her secondary school. The only disappointment was, she failed her GCSE core subjects.

Papa Joe was distraught. Chloe's failures were worsening an already sour relationship. She poured all her passion for serving the Saviour.

Directed through the many youth activities, she became involved in every event. Her commitment and love to the redeemer, coupled with her beauty and smile, soon attracted the opposite sex.

Nonetheless, her academic shortcomings frightened and crippled her. In order not to fail, she made a renewed vow to the lover of her soul and herself. She made Mama Joe her only confidant at sixteen years old.

Chloe's mother became her consultant for every man that passed through her life.

After church or wherever she went, she would come home and give her mother a detailed account. Who speaks to her, how he looked like, how he perceived her, and so on. Her mother was the best silent listener ever.

She never felt a need to criticise her and the choices she made. Mama Joe instead, encouraged her to speak to her Saviour about each man. She made her feel secure and provided a home for Chloe's troubled mind and her relationship with men.

Mama Joe went a step further to encourage her to bring her friends' home. She had no fears that her daughter would defile herself to suit the cravings of her emotions.

Mama Joe knew and trusted Chloe's commitment to her Saviour. She often opened her home, cooked and looked after the welfare of Chloe's friends. Mama Joe adopted each male friend introduced as her son.

With wisdom, Mama Joe watched from behind the scenes to understand the motive of each of them. The beautiful thing about her mother was that she prayed. Her prayers seemed to have guided Chloe all the way.

# A STEP INTO THE REAL WORLD

*Better a small serving of vegetables with
love than a fattened calf with hatred.*

A few months later, Papa Joe called Chloe into his room for a discussion.

"So, Chloe, what are we going to do about your failures, and this Saviour you claim you serve? Couldn't your Saviour help you pass?"

His disposition did not move Chloe to him. With a straight face, she replied,

"Papa, I would yet serve Him because my faith in Him is not dependent on my grades."

Furious with her candid response, Papa Joe rose from the side of his bed, opened the door in anger and said,

"Get out of my room. You vagabond! I do not want to have anything to do with you and your saviour forever."

Chloe resolved to pledge allegiance to the Cross. Her father had finally disowned her because of her faith. Nevertheless, she determined to make something out of her life - the first step was to start work.

She was now seventeen and still studying for her university entrance examination. She started working as a dispensary attendant for her neighbour. He had a critical illness and needed to keep the shop open.

The dispensary was five hundred yards next to the entrance of the University of the Ibadan. Opposite the university entrance is the Agbowo community.

The Agbowo community is known to be populated by off-campus students. Agbowo and all the businesses enjoyed the visibility of two monumental landmarks in Ibadan. Agbowo shopping complex skyscraper comprised the shopping hub for the students and the locals.

The second was the University of Ibadan tower. The hub, known to be the centre of the hustle and bustle of the university environment. It enjoyed the day and night busyness of economic transactions.

Loud music from different vendors and hawkers of various merchandise was a perfect description of the scenery. Agbowo was the place to be for every teenager, especially in the evenings. It was a beehive!

Chloe was excited about her first day of working independently in the shop. She dressed in her patterned ankara skirt and her light blue blouse.

Chloe's permed hair styled into a bob, crossed the road at a fast pace in the hot sun.

Suddenly, a Mercedes X class with black-tinted glass pulled up beside her. A voice beckoned to her from the window to approach the car.

In a friendly way, she walked over, thinking someone needed some directions.

Sloughed in the car was Mr Williams, an unpleasant memory plagued her. Her dance floor experience when she was ten years old.

She greeted in shock.

"Good morning, sir! Papa Joe is doing great. Have you been to his office or seen him today?"

Chloe did not wait for him to answer when she continued.

"Sir, I have to hurry to work. Today is my first day. I am running late."

Mr Williams was not a welcome guest in her mind. The sooner she got rid of him, the better.

She turned around to walk on, but Mr Williams reached out his hand and held hers. He said in a traditional accent,

"Chloe! Chloe, my wife;" laughing out obscenely he continued,

"Come and join me in the car and let's talk."

Chloe reflected on what she heard echoed to herself.

*"What! Okay, Mr Williams is my father's friend; he could have something important to say. But why should he call me a 'my wife?' Blood of Jesus!"*

Chloe reached for her phone, called her boss to inform him of a little delay on her way to work. She walked over to the passenger door, stepped into the back seat.

She was uncomfortable sitting with Mr Williams. Her intrusive brainwave puzzled within.

*"I need to hear what all this is about."*

Mr Williams stretched out his old wrinkled hands to hold her.

"You are a full-grown woman now! You know I have always had my eyes on you since you were a little damsel."

Chloe resisted his advances, but he continued.

"See, see, my love, I would follow all the right steps with Papa Joe. I won't do you any wrong; you are too special. I want to marry you. You would take the position of my third, no! My fourth wife."

Chloe shocked at the older man's foolish words, froze on the seat beside him. The shock had not bothered him, though raging anger displayed on her face. Instead, he intensified his efforts to woo her.

"Don't worry. You would never struggle again. I understand you have been having issues with your father. Marrying me would put you back into his good books."

His flirting escalated, as his hands moved from holding her hands to touching her face. Chloe shuddered. She raised her voice as she said:

"Mr Williams, I have known you since I was a child. But I am as a lock, stock and barrel disappointed as I was back then, even though I was little."

Her outburst shocked Mr Williams, and he immediately withdrew his hands. Her rant wasn't over.

"Sir or Mr Williams, whatever your name is. Any respect you could ever perhaps earn from me vanishes this very moment. I do not want you, your wealth or a position in your family. I recommend you go over to Papa Joe and tell him my exact words."

As she cantankerously stepped out of the car, she yelled,

"Shame on you! Do you indeed want to marry someone your daughter's age? You should repent now before you end up in hell."

Chloe slammed the door and walked off.

*"What a waste of space! Rubbish! Third or fourth wife? The fool doesn't even know the exact number of wives he has! Now I understand why Mama Joe prayed in silence that night; she knew a day like this would come!"*

Later in the evening, Chloe narrated the events of the day to Mama Joe. It was centred, especially on her encounter with Mr Williams. After they shared a time of intense laughter, Mama Joe spoke from her heart.

"Chloe, my child, I know I have loved you from the start and would always love you. I do not, in every respect, agree with your approach and response to Mr Williams. You insulted him, and that's not the Saviour's way. Remember His words. All you needed was a quiet and firm answer. Pray for him, and it would be easier for him not to end up in hell."

"Mama! I was rather pissed at the sight of the grumpy old man," Chloe replied.

"I am sorry, Mama," as she laid her head on her lap.

"You know what mother? I bet he would never come near me again."

"I bet you are right, my dear," Mama Joe replied, brushing her hair with composure.

*"I pray so,"* Chloe pondered in her heart.

The next Monday morning, it was raining cats and dogs, and Mama Joe was ill.

Chloe, torn between taking care of Mama Joe or going to work gazed to no avail at her mum. Mama Joe noticed that she was fighting in her thoughts, so she agreed that she had to get to work. After running through the showers of rain, Chloe got on the bus to work fair and square wet.

A young man boarded the bus and sat close to her. He kept staring at her until she cleared her throat and said,

"Can I help you?"

The young man, all of a sudden, stopped gazing. He spoke in the most fluent English accent she had ever heard:

"Sorry, I have seen no girl this beautiful before! Are you an angel? I am David."

The gentleman, who Chloe now identified as David continued to speak. He muttered with such unease:

"I am a student at the University of Benin. I came here to see my cousin at the University of Ibadan. Can I spend some time knowing this damsel?"

Not finished, he continued with,

"Has anyone told you how beautiful you are?"

Chloe was confident about her physical beauty apart from her teeth. She whispered,

"I know I am beautiful; an angel, I'm not. Also, my brothers compliment me at home. Being described as a beauty, it's not new for me."

The importance of speaking the right words into the ones we love, out of the blue, dawned on her.

A few moments later, she got off the bus with David. He kept talking as he walked alongside Chloe, who didn't give much attention to him.

Once they had walked past the gates of the university, she reminded him he had gone past where he was heading.

"I don't want this moment to end forever," David replied without a fight. Chloe smiled, and he responded with

"Look at those dimples!"

At the entrance of the shop, David assisted Chloe to pull up the metal security bars on the doors.

He watched as she talked to the Saviour, muttering her lips before she started on her daily activities. He seemed keen to help as she moved things from one place to the other.

She distracted herself from his engulfing eyes by reordering the medicines and other goods in the dispensary.

Customers soon came in and out to buy pills and bagged water popularly known as 'pure water'.

Smothered by David's eyes with every move she made, Chloe became uncomfortable. Besides, she seemed to enjoy knowing a guy fancied her beauty, from the corner of the room.

❀ ❀ ❀

An hour later, he excused himself and stepped out of the door. In relief, Chloe exhaled "

*Thank God! He could not get enough of this damsel. I hope David's gone for good? It's weird, in any case. How can he sit quietly for an hour and leave? Was his mission to admire me?"*

She had not finished the line of brainwave, when he walked back with some bags labelled Mr Biggs.

Mr Biggs was the latest restaurant in town. Smiling enthusiastically, he said,

"I didn't bother buying soft drinks because 1 know you sell here. I got snacks and ice creams."

"Sure, we do! Do you want to buy, and what drink would you like?"

"Would only buy drinks if you would join me."

"That's a hard bargain! Today is not one of those days; I feel or enjoy taking a drink."

After a random pause, she continued, "Let alone, eat."

"Why, what did I do? Do I irritate you that much?" He looked intensely at her, pleading for an answer.

Chloe's dimples gave way to an affectionate smile and replied, "No!"

"Not at all, didn't mean to sound rude. I would take mine later. I promise to take it. I would not want to mix business and pleasure."

Chloe could not admit she was fasting. She, however, felt so tempted to take up the offer to dine with him.

"Alright then," David seemed to have accepted her explanation.

"What drink should I serve you?"

"Do you have malt?"

"No, just soft drinks. Can I get you malt? If, that's what you want."

"It's okay; I'll take a bottle of coke," he replied with his enlarged pupils. He enjoyed his share of the snack alone. She watched undetected as he ate so politely.

*"His fingers are beautifully and wonderfully made. Whoa, this son of man looks rather good!"* she mulled over.

My mind is playing about again; she cautioned herself, focusing on her inventory.

Chloe enjoyed the moment and soaked up the admiration and the attention she had not received in a long time. It was at that moment that David said:

"Will you come and have a drink with me sometime?"

Chloe from nowhere came back to her senses and respectfully declined. He stood away from the chair where he sat.

David reached out his hands to hold hers; his hands felt so good, so soft and so succulent on her skin. She with no delay, let go of his hands.

"You are killing me, Chloe," he said with his eyes pleading.

She stood with no facial expression and replied,

"You make your choice."

David stayed in the pharmacy with her. He watched her for a while following her every move with his alluring eyes.

After several unsuccessful attempts at persuading her for a drink or her number, he left.

She right away flicked his image to the back of her mind and told herself,

"Sweet words cannot buy me on a shoestring".

*"Even though David looked like a pampered but amiable young man. He was a distraction and its regarded as one,"* she told herself.

David made such an impression on her. For the first time, she saw herself worthy of admiration by a young, handsome, privileged man.

His words kept ringing in her mind for days and weeks. She knew she would never see him again.

All she would remember and hold on to would be his name. David's impressive face with his touch; his voice and the soft kind words, he spoke to the most profound part of her heart.

Sometimes whenever her thoughts wandered to him, she wished she had got to know him more. She was sensing a need for someone special in her life after her encounter with David.

She knew she would put herself in a vulnerable position. Chloe considered all the challenges before her.

Loving the Saviour with all her heart, soul, and mind was her goal now.

## THE NEXT STEP

*A time to love and a time to hate,*
*a time for war and a time for peace.*

A few months after Chloe's encounter with David, the owner of the chemist, died. Heartbroken, she still had to work to sustain herself and her mother.

Her Papa Joe had finally cut out Mama Joe out of the family business. Being disowned by a father is not the most natural path to life for a teenager.

She fought the temptation to get what she needed from other means, like Mr Williams. But love still surrounded her, especially from Mama Joe.

Chloe sold snacks and drinks to make ends meet. On one occasion, she served a quiet, exhausted young man called Akin.

Though Chloe had forgotten her first encounter with him, this time, Chloe met him again at the local library where studying for her exams.

Chloe observed him better from the corner seat where she pretended to be studying.

Akin had a well-pronounced gap in his teeth. The feature daily announced itself with every smile that radiated from his face. His soft-spoken voice rang in Chloe's ears like the sound of quiet waters.

Even though she longed to chat with him, she never considered it her place to approach him. Instead, she waited well enough an encounter to bring them together once more.

Having done two hours reading, she stepped out of the library to stretch her legs.

Chloe walked over to buy groundnuts from a vendor beside the library. Without prior notice, she heard Akin's soft voice behind her saying,

"I know you. I have met you before."

Pretending she couldn't recollect, she responded:

"Don't you men say that to every girl you meet?"

Laughing at ease, he said,

"I am not men; from the bottom of my heart. I have met you before. Were you not the girl that served drinks at the Student Union building? What was a beautiful girl like you doing there? And what are you doing in the library? My name is Akin."

He, like greased lightning, realised he'd thrown a barrage of questions at her. Akin chuckled as he told Chloe his name.

Chloe broke the silence with her captivating smile. Her dimples were giving away her great delight. She replied Akin,

"Which of your questions do you want me to answer first?"

Akin laughed and said, "Anyone of them."

"Alright, I am reading for my university entrance examination. I am working to take care of my mother and myself."

Chloe could sense his shock from his changed countenance.

"How can a girl like you choose the hard choices?"
Reading his thoughts, she continued.

"Sometimes, life teaches lessons, and you have to learn the lessons to become a better person."
Akin smiled in a slurred voice.

"Don't you want to know me?"
Hiding her eagerness, she replied cheekily

"You tell me? Do you want me to know you?"
Akin with a peal of flirtatious laughter once again showing the gap in his teeth. Responded,

"I have gained admission to the Polytechnic. I was in the library to revise before heading for lectures."

Chloe continued to ask him questions. They shared jokes and talked for the remaining time they spent in the library.

Soon, it was time to go, and they walked home together. Chloe discovered that Akin lived two streets

away from Papa Joe's house. They agreed to go to the library together as often as possible.

The decision that soon flourished into a new and exciting relationship. Chloe confided in Mama Joe, and she looked forward to meeting the young man. She at the double added that she was not sure if they shared the same faith.

Chloe sensed something reserved Akin when she would question him about his faith. Chloe knew deep down that her relationship with Akin needed defining.

She was ruled by her faith, no matter how loud her emotions were screaming.

On their walk to the library one day Akin asked,
"Can we go to the botanical garden for a picnic?"

Chloe's heart skipped at the thought of spending time alone with him. Although it was not the first, she would spend time with her male companions.

It was the first time with someone who made her pulse race faster. She tried to change the tone of the discussion, but Akin was adamant about continuing.

"You have not given me a reply yet."

He turned his inquiry eyes on her.

Clearing her throat in discomfort, she said,

"Sure, I hope we wouldn't take too long? I didn't tell Mama Joe."

"Ehh! Mama Joe, she would be fine. You are a big girl now. I bet you can take care of yourself, can't you?"

"Sure, I can. What do you take me for?"
Chloe smiled, looking away from his piercing gaze all over her.

"Okay, let me make it easier. We could leave the library earlier today, so that you can get back to your Mama Joe, at your usual time."

Chloe, surprised by his kind consideration, shook her head in approval.

"That would be good," she muttered.

"But wait! What are we eating? Where is the food basket?"

Akin reached out his palm to her.

"Touch it," he said.

"Trust... believe. I would make all the provisions happen. All I need is a Yes."

"Yes," Chloe said, smiling with her pinched lips walking ahead of him into the library.

After two hours of staring into her books, she gave up; her mind imagined what the afternoon would be like with Akin. It excited a part of her; It scared the other of crossing the boundaries.

She reassured herself, *"It would be an open space, don't be afraid."*

Tapping his feet under the table restlessly, she signals to him. It was time to leave. Chloe packed her books and walked out of the library. Akin walked out without a sound after her.

Once outside, they laughed together as they strolled towards the botanical garden.

The weather was sunny and hot. There were few people on the street; it was around midday and folks were out and about.

She prayed that no familiar faces would notice her. She dreaded a confrontation at home. The trust Mama Joe had with her was on a test.

All she could think was the moments they would share.

They arrived at the entrance after twenty minutes of walking. Akin's little cousin greeted them, carrying a small woven basket.

"Brother Akin, here is the basket you asked me to bring. I have been waiting for an hour now."

"Thank you," Akin replied, retrieving the basket from him. "Now run back home, your work here is completed, run along!"

"Aunt Chloe, good afternoon. I hope you enjoy my big brother's company."
He prostrated half-way as he walked away.

"I will," she replied. "My greetings to big mummy," she added as he exited their presence.

They found a well-shaded spot under a tree. Akin spread the cloth, while she waited for an invitation to sit.

Akin, like the gentleman, invited her to sit beside him. Chloe couldn't believe he could make her so special as she imagined.

She felt relaxed as the cool breeze blew beneath her exposed legs. Akin's tender attitude towards her charmed her.

The afternoon went so well; they discussed their time in school. Although Chloe did most of the talking, Akin was a great listener.

Their walk home was awkward without explanation. Akin seems to want to hold her hands; she was conservative and felt at odds with grasping hands.

She felt a touch might make her lose her peace with the Saviour. The turbulent Chloe felt inside was worse than a raging sea.

She felt choked with the thought of doing something wrong. Chloe sensed that Akin wanted more than a simple goodbye. Her heart screamed within,

"What does he want?"
Chloe did not want to mess up the reminiscences of the lovely afternoon. In discomfort, she looked away from his sparkling eyes and muttered:

"Have a good evening."

She hurried into the house like a speed of light and raced to the window. Chloe watched the poor fellow from inside her house.

She felt sorry for him. He stood heartbroken, wondering what he had done wrong. After some minutes, he put himself together and walked off.

The next day, they communicated with each other as usual. They pretended there was never an odd moment between them.

A few days later, on the way from the library, Akin invited Chloe to try out his favourite snack. Akin had spoken about it like something so special that she could not imagine it.

They had a walk to the vendor close to his house selling this unique snack. Chloe still curious like she was as a little girl, agreed to try it out. Her throat was salivating to taste this unknown mouth-watering described grub.

After walking forty-five minutes from the library, enjoying a friendly chat, they approach the older woman.

To her surprise, the renowned snack was "Boli and Epa" – roasted plantain and groundnut.

Chloe laughed so much if it was the last time she had to. "Haha! Haa. Is this the well-endowed snack you described? You are such a fake guy! How is this special?"

She questioned his notion of the 'special' phrase.
Akin laughing pleasantly as his usual self-replied,

"Chloe, you need to taste, this woman's version, it differs completely from whatever you know before."
Expressing his open gap tooth, Chloe now looked forward to whenever he smiled.

"Really, for real? Perhaps eating this version with you would make a distinct difference."

"Now, you are talking!" He laughed as he paid for the purchase.

They walked to the nearby field to enjoy the snack. It was true; it not necessarily the food that needs to be perfect. The person you eat the food with makes all the difference.

Every moment with Akin was different. Perhaps, it differed from what she often knew. Her friends in church were not the same; his company had a special touch to her heart. She was afraid to understand it. She wanted to enjoy every moment.

Chloe invited Akin to meet her mother the next day. Mama Joe was kind as usual, welcoming him with warmth into their home. He thoughtfully commended her kindness and her delicious food.

Every day, Chloe was looking forward to the walks to the library together with Akin. Oh! The joy of talking and laughing.

Knowing that he would soon leave for college, she was keen to make the most of the time she had with him. Things went so fast within a short time, and one evening when they were together, Akin like a shot asked:

"Chloe, would you like to go out with me?"

Admitting, Chloe was enjoying his company. She was not expecting any question relating to a committed relationship.

Fear gripped her stomach! Chloe cleared her tight throat and said,

"Can I consider it?"

Akin, so sure of himself with his happy face, said,

"Take your time, not too long. I am leaving for college soon."

Holding her hands, Chloe filled with mixed feelings, nodded with a

"Yes, sure."

At home that evening, Chloe withdrew, and Mama Joe could not reach her.

Chloe tried to pray, but she was so confused about her daring emotions.

*"How can I like him? I can't have him. Am I not too young? I'm too vulnerable to understand what to do, right!"*

Everything about Akin was too much for Chloe, who was only a few weeks from her nineteenth birthday. Amid the discontentment in her heart, the gentle voice of the Saviour spoke.

**"I have loved you with an everlasting love. I gave you the emotions. I can handle it."**

Soon she felt a fresh assurance and boldness to deal with the situation. She, like a flicker, stood up, took a sheet of paper and began to write to Akin.

*Dear Akin,*
*I appreciate my friendship with you, and if truth be told, I would love to take it to the next level. Though, I am worried that we are not on the same page.*
*My faith is the foundation of my life, and I base all my choices on my faith. Even though I would have loved to take you up on your offer, I know it would hurt Jesus. The lover of my soul as we do not have a common understanding of my faith. I*
*would love you to have an encounter with my lover. You would never regret it. I*
*would still be your friend if you would have me, but I can't go to the next step with you.*
*Thank you and much appreciated.*
*Chloe,*
*Your friend*

Chloe handed Akin the letter the next day. Although Akin's reactions were not noticeable, she was sure he would have misunderstood her.

Chloe had decided. Shop closed and gone out of business until she was confident about his stance, with the Saviour.

Akin left for college without a goodbye. Chloe remained a faithful friend to him. No matter what happens, she would always welcome the decisions he made. She knew in every respect, well; she still had a soft spot for him

# FIRST MOVE

*For the creation was subjected to frustration,
not by its own choice, but by the will of the one
who subjected it, in hope.*

Akin seemed to have vanished. She missed the company of her friend. She would sometimes walk past his house, as her heart longed to speak to him.

Sadly, Chloe's faith went through one test to another, shaping her resolve to remain with her Lover and Saviour. Her relationships with the opposite sex did not go untested.

Even though she loved the Lord, she was unsure about how to deal with her failures. Foremost, her education. She immersed herself in church and pastoral activities.

Chloe was using activities to block out the responsibility to deal with the little girl within her.

She became very active with the youth prayer group. She committed to seeing the love of the Saviour birthed in others.

The youth group was essential and a pleasant place to be. Being part of the group faded away from the encompassing thoughts of the missed company with Akin. The community became an extended family for her.

Chloe started developing other healthy relationships. Chloe's friendliness made her a well-known figure amidst the young and the old.

She related to the older group because of her depth of wisdom and knowledge. Her maturity over a short timeframe spurred out of hard-line experiences.

Within the community, they described her as daring, reliable and trusting a contrast to her childhood. But sometimes too gullible in believing people and accepting their views.

Mama Joe raised her, to be honest, and straightforward like the Saviour expect her to be. She was naïve to believe the world was flat, pure as they raised her to think the community should be.

One evening during the fellowship, it was thanksgiving time. Chloe remembered an incident she had told no one. When it was her turn to share, she recalled what happened one night.

An episode that occurred while she was in the boarding house.

There was an ongoing rumour that a male spirit or man comes into the dormitory. He flirts with the girls while they were asleep. As it was a rumour, she did not believe.

There were other stories of other strange incidences with no evidence; this was like any other. The dormitory was the largest in the hostel with fifty beds. Many of whom were junior girls.

Chloe was one of the ten senior lassies, each positioned at several points in the hall. Light out was eight pm, and the girls ought to be in bed.

Chloe usually sleeps like a baby; However, that night, she seemed to have a restless sleep. The location of her bunk bed at the end of the hall. They advised each student to keep a touch under their pillow just in case of an emergency.

As rumour has it, the stranger comes in from the entrance. He moves from one bunk to another with a tiny touch to view the half-naked girls on their beds, especially the girls without underwear.

A little after one am, she heard the door to the hall opening, at first Chloe anticipated it was one of the girls going out to the toilet. But since the rumour started, the girls avoided going out at night. Somewhat, improvised means, toileting without going out using bowls and old buckets.

The steps moved a bunk at a time using a touch light to look into the beds. It was so creepy to watch the movement of the figure.

*"It was true! The girls were not lying about it. I need to do something."*

By the time she felt the movements in the middle of the hallway, she had switched into action. Padding her hands under her pillow, she took hold of her touch light.

Little by little, she lifted the mosquito net covering her bed. In a swift action, she shouted racing behind him.

"Who are you? What do you want here? You don't belong here."

Once on her feet, the stranger ran out of the room, while the girls screamed:

"Senior Chloe, senior Chloe, don't go, please don't go after the stranger."

Chloe did not realise many of the girls kept watch at night. The staff and students commented Chloe for her bravery, but she knew her help came from the Saviour.

The whole school accepted a stranger was coming into the boarding house.

They beefed the security up for the safety of the girls. Some parents, however, withdrew their kids from the boarding house.

Chloe got the nickname "Senior Chloe" from the community. She enjoyed the attention and though seemed to overly trusting with critical thinking.

Chloe still harboured a sense of rejection from her childhood. She longed for a special friend she would open that part of her too.

She felt vulnerable, sharing her most profound feeling. The daily challenges were enough to overshadow the need for acceptance.

As the fellowship grew, clicks were forming of individuals. She wanted someone she could relate with like Akin, but it seemed everyone had no emotions running in their veins.

A click relationship was something Chloe was not a comfortable niche for her. There was a growing trend of the marriage proposals amongst the group.

Therefore, the dilemma created a problematic space for Chloe to mingle in at nineteen-years-old.

She was not ready to be a man's woman or for being his wife. Chloe wanted friendship and nothing much with it. She watched others, especially the older youths picking each other.

She also noticed a general trend. It was difficult for the brothers; if the ladies declined their proposals. She could only imagine what was going on in the mind of these men.

They deemed a rejected proposal a failure: a default, or their inability to hear the Saviour's voice in particular.

*"Does the Saviour, speak to them? Does He, in detail, state one lady for a particular guy? Do I have a choice to make?"*

Chloe asked herself in a rare brainwave. These were some questions she could not fit into her ideology. Her idea was to meet a guy, know him for who he is first.

Pray and look forward to him asking her out or something like that. Without a doubt, this did not involve pursuing him.

It was so traditional and rigid that Chloe dreaded the moment anyone would approach her. What would she do or say? *"I am not into these ideas,"* Chloe told herself.

Her friends would be friends for now; anyone that wants her would have to wait until she is READY.

Many of the young men of similar age to her in church soon became familiar faces in her home. They were already in the university, and her home was an oasis to rest after the stress of lectures.

Although Chloe had fun with all her friends, she did not deem anyone's attraction as a promise of a relationship. Frank and Luke visited almost every so often.

Frank lived a few miles from her home and was from a humble family. Frank's heritage drove him to make his life more of a success than his parents.

Frank was a short man with dark skin and like peas in a pod clockwork lousy mouth odour. His physical appearance did not affect the way she related to him.

Mama Joe had always told her that physical presence was not a judge of good human character.

Frank was a well-known brother in the prayer group that Chloe was committed. He had an excellent command of the Saviour's words.

By Chloe's assessment, he prayed a lot and seemed to love the Saviour. Traits that other people, including herself, respected and admirer in him. He would encourage Chloe, especially when she was low. Fighting temptation and not living like the rest of her mates.

In her struggle with Papa Joe, Frank always had the right words from the 'good book'. She regarded him as a special brother and treated him so.

One cold, breezy evening after a prayer meeting in the church, he tapped her shoulder. Frank informed Chloe that he had something important to discuss with her.

As usual, she expected it would be the words of encouragement from the Saviour. His words, Chloe never took without due consideration.

An older member had planned to drop off Chloe at home, but she was in the company of Frank. Chloe declined the invitation for a drive home and chose to walk.

She knew it would take one to two hours to walk home together, with Frank's spiritual aptitude and company.

Halfway into their walk, Frank started referring to the Saviour's words. To her amazement from a different perspective.

His persuasive words and gestures created a strange discomfort in Chloe's mind, but she continued the walk with him. As they approached the gate to her house, he made a direct statement her.

"Chloe, God said you are my wife!"

He stated with confidence "that God had in its entirety told him He meant her to be his wife."

Chloe knew this was an ongoing trend in their fellowship. She had communicated her thoughts about this with few people, including Frank.

Chloe was not expecting it would happen to her so soon! She was only nineteen years old. How would Chloe run away from this moment?

On the contrary, it was what she had dreaded most!

*"Wife? Wife? That was the last thing on Chloe's mind. Not even a girlfriend! Whoa, whoa, whoa! Where did that come from, His wife? "*

Her heart was spinning as her heartbeat was racing. The only thing she wanted to do was to run into the house. Chloe replied, trembling.

"I need time to consider your proposal, Frank. You know that I was not expecting to be in a relationship soon."

Frank looked away for a moment and said,

"Chloe, take as much time as you want."

His words seemed more of a grumble and nothing like his confident declaration. Chloe bid him "goodnight," with quick steps into the house in search of Mama Joe.

Okay! Chloe understood the viewpoint that God was coming into the debate. It was usual for a young man to say God has said that they should marry a lady.

The lady then goes to pray about it and gives a response of yes or no.

It was often 'yes' with the consideration that God would have confirmed to the lady she was to be his wife. In Chloe's case, it was a rude awakening.

Marriage was the last idea on the mind of this young lady. She had not passed her exams to gain admission to the university.

Frank was already in the university, and she was not ready to open the book of marriage. Without wasting his time, she planned to tell him that God was not directing her.

She believed certain things had to be with certainty in a place first. For instance, her academics, before even considering marriage.

Chloe was angry and frustrated. She felt Frank had destroyed their 'pure' friendship, introducing God's demand on her to marry him.

*"How could he do this to me? How, how? I am not ready,"* she screamed to herself.

She had a lengthy discussion with her mother. Mama Joe understood Chloe's perspective of wanting the best for herself.

She wished she had opportunities while growing up to make those choices for herself. Her mother was married off as a thirteen-year-old girl to her father.

Mother would support her choice of timing, which she never had. Mama Joe held up her daughter through the difficult times ahead.

Three days after his proposal, Frank came up to Chloe after the service asking for an answer to his marriage proposal.

*"He is looking his best this morning,"* she reflected. Frank wore the usual native clothing, and it had become a regular scene to see him in the same old iron pressed attire.

He was rather excited as if he had uncovered a pot of gold. Chloe, in spite of this, filled with mixed feelings.

She wished he would leave her alone for a few months to work through her emotions. To get a clear mind to seek the Saviour.

Did Frank expect an answer after three days? Would Chloe have a well-prepared positive response for him?

Chloe explained,

"Frank, I need more time. I do not think I have the answer at the moment."

She sensed an overwhelming pressure from him to give him an answer. Because he re-emphasised that he had heard God speak to him. Frank responded,

"How much time do you need?"

Chloe already agitated, chivalrously replied,

"I am not sure."

But Frank was not happy with this unnecessary delay. You could sense his impatience in his voice and body language.

Feeling confused, Chloe, in due course, said "NO," which did not go down well.

The relationship between Frank and Chloe slowly but surely turned sour. Although she first related to him as usual, her attitude soon became cold.

She wanted to erase the thoughts of Frank, but it was not an easy task. Chloe could not avoid the gossips and the bitterness from others in the fellowship.

She felt alone. Does the Saviour, in reality, want her to be betrothed and to be married? When she was not even sure where her next meal would appear like falling stars.

Chloe was glad she had an understanding mother awaiting her back home.

Mama Joe could not answer all her questions, although She often told Chloe, "The answer lays within your heart; listen with awareness."

Months later, Chloe's friendship with Luke had blossomed. She kept company with him more often than usual. Luke was approachable and understanding of her views on Frank's proposal.

He was less aggressive and was lovely being around him. He was a good listener and would only respond when he needed to. This trait endeared him to her if truth be told.

She would talk for hours while he listened. Chloe weighed,

*"Luke would be a better person to ask me out, only at the right time."*

Other times, Chloe would visit Akin's hoping to find out if he was home. He seemed not to visit from college, which was strange. She missed his company.

# ANOTHER WORLD

*Because of the Lord's great love, we are not consumed,*
*for his compassions never fail.*

Mama Joe was fond of Luke, and she encouraged their friendship. He was from a humble background.

Even though his perspective on life, God, and success differed from Frank's.

Chloe often looked forward to Luke's company. Most times, once he'd finished his class a few miles away from Chloe's house, he would walk to Chloe's. They would spend time together gardening.

They teased each other and shared pondered about each other's family and the effect on their lives. Luke used the opportunity to ask her to cross-examine his level of understanding. She questioned him on his medical courses.

The most exciting subject to Chloe was Anatomy. Chloe knew she would have loved to be a doctor. But she had taken social science subjects in secondary school.

It would be a tight switch for her. Apparently, she was glad her friends could accomplish much more than she could.

Chloe soon developed ways of playing pranks with Luke. She found this funny, though she knew this did not always go down well with him. His blinking eyes always gave him away when upset.

One Saturday morning, he dropped by for breakfast at Chloe's on his way to his tutorial classes and test.

Unknown to him, she went into Luke's bag and took his Anatomy textbook for her usual pranks.

After breakfast, Luke headed out fast because he was running late. Not realising, he had left something behind.

Halfway to his destination, Chloe texted Luke to check he had all he needed. Only then, did he discover that she had played her usual tricks on him.

He turned back upset, running all the way, sweating and blinking his eyes. Chloe felt rather horrible for letting her dear friend go through the stress, early in the morning.

Though she apologised again later, Luke refused to talk about the incident. His reply was,

"It's okay. Keep having fun! That's what you do".

Chloe learnt a valuable lesson. Even though it's okay to have fun, you mustn't have fun at the expense of another person.

Painfully, she later found out he was late for the test that morning.

Luke developed his relationships with others in the university. He is causing a strain that affected their relationship.

Initially, Chloe did not allow these relationships to change her by accepting his friends like hers. She raised no objections nor appeared to be possessive of him.

Chloe did not want him to see her through the insecurity ravaging her existence. So, she withdrew a little at a time, from Luke and his friends.

Chloe pretended she was not going through an emotional roller-coaster. Acting actively outside but broken within in the absence of her dear friends.

She developed a friendship with a co-worker in her new job, where she worked as a team coordinator.

Femi was great at anything he did. In his expertise and to his credit, Femi knew how to turn on her female side. With him, she was ultimately herself. She soon lost herself in friendship with him.

There was no conflicting academic difference between them. Femi was already a biochemist. Chloe soon filled the vacuum Akin, and Luke had created, with the attention Femi poured on her.

The annual three days team retreat seemed like a magical place to put all her troubles behind for a few days. It's aimed at improving the working relationship with the rest of the group.

In Chloe's mind, a chance to know Femi more. She needed to figure out why he was so likeable. Or perhaps, annoy him to test his "elasticity." Why does everyone find him so reliable?

It was Chloe's first-time experience of village living, with its pure simplicity. The venue was two hours away from the city to the village.

The journey was bumpy because of the untarred road and dust blowing in the air. Chloe covered her nose with a scarf while struggling to breathe; to reduce the amount of dust, coming through the windows.

Once at the venue, there was an uproar. It thrilled the few children to have visitors from the city amongst them.

Some offered to carry their luggage to their lodgings; this was handy for Chloe – the journey exhausted her.

The first day was busy. There was no electricity; they prepared meals with firewood.

They divided the group into two. One group gathered the wood needed, and the other proceeded to the stream for water.

Chloe, like Mama Joe, enjoyed cooking, and she joined the cooking team. The team cleaned up at the creek.

All the ladies headed out first, at their return, all the men. By the last event of the day, they were all exhausted and ready for bed.

The night did not go as expected; The mosquitoes bites were like an army invading new territory. She tossed from side to side wishing it was daylight.

She laid awake by the noise of the crickets, chirping with their annoying stridulating sounds. There seemed to be a competition between some ladies snoring level and the noise outside.

By the early hours of the morning, she became tired and yearned for her bed. Chloe rose out before the cock crowed, though most were still sleeping.

She stepped out of the hut. The breath of fresh air was remarkable.

Chloe took a walk into the forest. Making her way through the trees and shrubs, she communed with the Saviour. From a distance, she saw Femi already gathering wood.

"Such a hard worker! He is always thinking about serving others, not surprising others find him reliable."

"Morning!" Chloe called out to him.

Even though he bent over, he replied with no doubt.

"Morning, Chloe, did you sleep well? If I know you, I guess you did not."

"How would you know that? Does it mean a princess can't adapt to new environments? Wait! How did you know it was me? You were not even looking up?"

She quizzed with smiles beaming to acknowledge a dear friend.

"I can recognise your voice even in my dreams,"

Femi with gusto responded. He adjusted his position to sit underneath the huge oak tree.

"Don't you reasonable like the simplicity of village living?", he continued.

"I do, but it's not for me. For starters, that means I won't ever sleep at night for the joys of nightcrawlers and mosquitoes."

"Hee! Hee," He laughed.

"Not for me. A visit would be sound fine. But if the convenience of the city is here, I may well reconsider."

She said, sliding beside him as they chatted.

Other members of the team soon found them. They advised them to join the rest of the group. The day rolled by without delay. With all the planned activities, there was no time for side-talks with Femi.

She was not looking forward to the night in the hut.

1.00 am the second night, Chloe concluded there was no point lying down in the dark. She would light lit a lantern and sit outside to read.

She stepped out in situ between the ladies sleeping on the mattresses. Chloe tiptoed, unlocking the door to step out.

"Aaaahh! What are you doing here?"
She exclaimed with her heart leaping off her shoulder.

"What are you doing here? Are you not supposed to be sleeping in the male quarters? You are in front of the ladies' quarters, can you explain yourself?"

"Pssshh! Keep quiet and sit down beside me; don't wake up anyone. I would explain,"

Femi protested, muttering in silence.
Chloe sat beside him, discontented,

*"This is weird. Is this guy abnormal or what? Does he have a motive for doing this? First, I saw him in the forest alone at dawn, and now he is alone in the middle of the night. Ahh! In fact! he must have a good explanation, or I would scream."*

She held on fast to her wrapper in terror. Chloe fought her spearing thoughts, replacing every right image about him to evil.

"Don't get defensive on me, Chloe!" Femi said.

"The men are taking turns to guard the ladies' huts. Yesterday, we got communications that a few months ago, there was a robbery in the village."

"We had to make sure you ladies were safe. Someone else would come out in the next thirty minutes to take over from me."

"Does any of the ladies know about the robbery?"
She protested with her eyeballs bulging out in disbelief.

"Of course! A few knew. They agreed not to let everyone know, in order not to cause a panic. We'll be here for only two nights; there was no point heading back to the city." He continued,

"That's the reason I was in the forest this morning. I was amongst the team guarding the forest last night."

"Do you mean your men didn't sleep? What if there was an attack? How would we have managed?"

"In real fact," Femi replied.

"But we made sure we kept the ladies safe first. The plan was to scare them off, all being well. I don't think village thieves are as sophisticated as the ones in the city."

Chloe relaxed, thought to herself,

"Real men protect their women with no fuss about it. He is a real man!"

They talked for about fifteen minutes. As Femi informed her earlier, a brother showed up with a lantern to relieve him of his duty.

They exchanged pleasantry. Femi and Chloe took a walk under the moonlight to the nearby field.

"It so cool to be outside. The night is breath-taking here. How I wish one of these stars would drop on my hands."

Chloe said, sitting on the grass while pulling Femi to sit beside her. Femi seemed reluctant at first but obliged her company after she persisted.

Femi sat without interruption and watched her talk on and on until she said,

"Femi, do you want to sleep?"

"As a matter of fact! I am not feeling sleepy. In reality, since you came out of the hut, I lost the need to sleep," Femi replied, laughing.

Chloe amused the utterance on the upshot she had on him, lifted the lantern to his face,

"Femi, that's not funny! Are you serious?"

Chloe blushed in denial on the effect she has on others by shuffling her feet and biting her nails.

"Yes, I am serious;" he replied.

Femi laid down beside Chloe with confidence like someone who merited the gold price.

"Tell me, why didn't you respond at all, I truthful went on and on."

Femi laughed at the statement she made; on and on and on and said:

"Chloe, I enjoy listening to you and having your company. I need not say anything."

Chloe inches by inches laid down beside him watching the stars. "I enjoy your company too," she told herself.

"We can remain here for the rest of our lives if possible," feeling relaxed and hanging on every word spoken by Femi.

Chloe hands flirtatious reached out to Femi's in response to her thoughts. Her heavy breathing, accompanied by a racing pulse.

Femi responded to her trembling hands. His warm, strong hands were covering hers with great comfort.

"Chloe! To what extent do you want someone to go with you before crossing your boundaries?"

Femi replied, holding his breath to resist the moment they shared recently.

Chloe pinched her lips in shame, released her hands from his grip.

"I'm sorry I made you feel uncomfortable. I did not intend for that to happen. Yet, it's true; things can get tricky, quick. I have defined my boundaries. No matter what happens, I have pledged the Saviour. My private places remain sequestered."

"Until I - Chloe without protest, present it to my husband."

Femi readjusted himself with his face focusing on her still lying down.

"What are your private places, lady?" he asked with his curious look.

"Leave me alone, silly!" Chloe giggled, Femi laughed in response.

"My private place is any part of the body my clothes covers. Not to spell it out to you, you know already, but with interest, it includes my mouth."

"Your mouth?" Femi interrupted giggly,

"That's serious. It would be a very tough bargain, especially during the period of engagement. "

"Yes! My mouth," she replied, laughing and hitting his chest spiritedly.

"You know, I like this playful part of you. Keep it a treasure for your husband. He would love you for it."

"Thank you, Femi; you would get to know him one day," she laughed.

"Right, I added my mouth, because once that boundary crossed, you are on a free run to nowhere."

"What do you mean nowhere? It's defined, we all know where it would lead."

They both laughed hysterically. Femi and Chloe continued to talk until Chloe yawning, placed her head on his board shoulder, and slept off.

Femi slowly but surely used his feet to move her blanket to cover her legs. He pondered,

"Chloe had become such an important part of me, yet she can't be mine."

# BAGGING UP THE EMOTIONS

*No one can serve two masters. Either you
will hate the one and love the other, or you will be devoted to
the one and despise the other.*

Isn't it funny how some people do not give up? Eight weeks after Chloe refused Frank's marriage proposal, he approached her again. She had taken time out to talk to the Saviour about his request.

She had searched her heart and realised they did not share much in common. Many of her friends enjoyed doing stuff together. They enjoy playing, gardening, fishing, and cooking.

Apart from spiritual commitments, they didn't share any downtime. It bothered Chloe.

She realised that relationships go beyond faith talk and that it was okay to look at reality too. She needed a friend as much as a spiritual partner.

Chloe tried to avoid him and yet, after service one Sunday, Frank hurried after her. He called out,

"Sister Chloe, Sister Chloe!"

It was embarrassing because she did not want to talk to him. Secondly, she really didn't like to be referred to as sister. Chloe simply wanted to be called "Chloe."

He asked to speak with her behind closed doors, and they walked to the nearby fig tree.

At first, she tried to make him understand. She was not ready for any long-term relationship.

But Frank wanted to keep her in a tight corner by insisting that it was a divine providence of God. She had no other choice.

This time Chloe flared up. She told him never to raise the topic with her again.

Chloe reached out to hug him, but Frank was too rigid to receive it. She walked away non-stop while he stood frozen.

Chloe told Mama Joe about the nightmare experience she had with Frank. It confused her. Even if God had spoken to him, he should consider that God has also given her a 'will' and 'time' to follow her heart.

In annoyance, she voiced her failures and the need to focus on passing her exams. An utter mismatch!

Mama Joe advised Chloe not to give her friends a lousy impression. She should not make a scene even though she was not ready to have a committed relationship with Frank.

Mama Joe said,

"Chloe, you need to work on your anger. Patient and quiet answers would achieve better results."

To which Chloe responded,

"Thank you, Mama, please pray for me."

Three months after the encounter with Frank, Luke approached. There had been an unexplained vacuum between them. Chloe's impression was

*"He wants to make up for lost times with me!"*

However, to her amazement, he proposed marriage. It was devastating.

If only he had not walked away from her with his new friends at university. He had no clue what she had suffered.

She longed for his company, and he disappeared only to reappear for "marriage sake!"

*"For heaven's sake, what is wrong with these brethren? Can we enjoy friendships without labels?"*

The situation confused Chloe.

*"I liked Luke, but does he not understand? It would never be the same ... wrong timing! Wrong timing..."*

Mama Joe was sad. She liked Luke, but she knew Chloe - once she had set a standard for herself, she seemed unbendable like a rock.

Mama Joe said nothing about it; As an adult, she left Chloe to make her own decisions. It was not long before Chloe dared to discuss with Luke.

She arranged a visit with Luke in her garden, their favourite place.

It was a sunny day with the trees providing the shade they needed. She made a lovely meal of rice and beans.

They ate together with joyful pleasure.

They remembered the promises of the Saviour. They were reassuring themselves of His plan for their lives.

After the meal, Chloe reached out and held Luke's hands. Looking intensely into his eyes, she said,

"Lukkii! Luke, you know I like you and would want to be with you. I do not feel that I can be in a relationship. My priority is not getting engaged now. I would have to decline your proposal at the moment."

Luke still holding on to Chloe's hands, replied,

"I... I... I thought we could move our friendship to the next level. I... I am sorry, I asked... can I take it back?".

Chloe's eyes swollen with tears pushed Luke's head on her shoulder and said,

"No, you can't. Nothing would change our friendship from my side. It's bad timing".

Chloe felt sorry she had to say 'No.'

Her reasons did not differ from what she had told Frank. Once she gets into the university, like all her suitors, she would decide accordingly.

Chloe, to a great extent, hoped that Luke would understand her reasoning.

He was a very dear friend, with a special place in her heart. She knew him; she realised him for herself, and she knew when Luke was happy or sad.

She knew the right questions to use to coax him into speaking his feelings, even though he is a man of few words.

Chloe tried to make Luke reason with her. To her surprise, Luke narrated her response to his close friends.

Their reactions resulted in unexpected and indirect bullying. They concluded that Chloe had been insensitive towards him.

Chloe was tenaciously devastated. The feedback she gave tormented her because she liked him straight up.

Chloe knew the only place to run was the hands of the Saviour. She spoke to Him day and night, taking comfort in the unwavering promises of His words.

*"Should I now say yes?"*

Chloe questioned her decision each day.

To her amazement, she found out that Luke got affianced to another lady. About two months after he had asked her out.

She pondered,

*"Wow! No mourning period?"*

On the one hand, it irritated her that Luke took their friendship for granted. On the other, she asked herself,

*"Did he in actuality have true feelings for me, the same way I had for him?"*

Chloe did not bother to wait for an answer. It's goodbye; the door closed!

She tried to remain friends with him as much as possible, learning from the experience she had with Frank.

One part of her often questioned the influence of Luke's friends on his behaviour toward her. That would be a question impossible to answer.

She would instead let sleeping dogs lie. She felt worn out and ardently scattered.

✿ ✿ ✿

Chloe relied on Femi for comfort; he had become fond of her. They began to spend all the spare time they had together.

Although he was older than her, compared to Luke and Frank, he was much more understanding.

He seemed to have much wisdom to answer any question she had.

She knew they would not take it beyond friendship. Yet, attracted to each other. Chloe's relationship with Femi was her greatest emotional battle ever.

The attention she never got from Papa Joe, Femi gave her. Although she was almost willing to do anything, the fear of the Saviour created a barrier for her.

She told herself the Saviour would turn His back on her if she tried to kiss Femi not to talk of having detailed intimate with him.

She hated the idea that she could be the one that would cause a beloved brother to fall into fornication.

Chloe did not want to an ugly history hanging over her head. She was finding it difficult to discuss her struggles with Mama Joe.

One morning on her way to work, Mama Joe said,

"Chloe, keep your mind and actions focused on the right things. There is a war raging inside you. I know it even if you don't tell me. I am praying for you."

Chloe walked over to her mother, who was sitting on the sofa, held her hands and replied,

"Mama, don't worry, I can handle it. If I am losing it, I will run straight into your hands."

Chloe knew she was not locked, stock and barrel honest with her.

"I should have been honest with Mama; she cares," Chloe mused.

Mama Joe watched over her with jealousy.

On one occasion, after staring into each other's eyes. Femi said,

"I would give you a new name because of what you have done in my life."

Chloe listened as she held out her hand to hold his. Smiling, he continued,

"You are my melody because you bring melody and have made my life melodious since I met you."

"You are such a romantic!" Chloe exclaimed.

Chloe desperately wanted to kiss him. She rose, gave him a peck and said:

"Goodnight. I can't handle this."

Chloe escaped from whatever would have happened that night.

As she walked home alone, his words kept ringing in her mind. Chloe reminded herself.

*"That any wrong move could have led her down the road, she had vowed never to walk without her husband".*

Tears dropped from her eyes as she remembered Mama Joe's words.

"There is a war raging inside you."

She began to sing praises to the Saviour to keep her mind in check.

For the next couple of months, she became more than usually depended on Femi. Also, gossip had gone out that they were more than casual friends.

Chloe became terrified of her feelings. Unable to cope with the scandals, she ran to her mother.

Mama Joe reassured her, letting her know that she believed in her. And her ability to stay pure as her Saviour would expect.

She knew it was time to handle it. They had to talk about it.

The question was, how far could she go without crossing the boundaries? Femi and Chloe had an adult chat about boundaries.

"Femi, do you remember we had a conversation about boundaries? I mean, the Boundaries! I need to keep, during the workers' retreat?"

Chloe questioned with a serious expression on her face as they shared his dinner. Surprised by the line of questioning, Femi replied,

"Yes."

He stared into the bowl of rice and beans, one of his favourite meals without looking at her.

Chloe placed her hands on his hand that was resting on the table.

"Look into my eyes. I am not accusing you of anything. I am as responsible for my actions as you are. Femi, we need a new approach to our friendship. Chloe like you, but we are not a thing."

Femi, though, minimising eye contact, stooped his shoulders in agreement.

"Melody, I see you from the perceptive of an unresolved big brother. I have not felt like this about any woman."

Chloe nodded in agreement with his affirming statement. She fidgeted with her clothing.

"As friends, we are attracted to each other deep down, but I don't know what the future holds for you. You don't want a committed relationship. Even if you want commitment, it should not be higgledy-piggledy with intense passion. Although I am ready for a relationship, I don't have all it takes to take care of you yet." He concluded.

Chloe replied,

"Don't say that Femi. Every woman would want you. It doesn't matter whether you are rich; you have a heart of gold."

Femi looked into her eyes penetratingly.

"You are too kind!"

Looking away, trembling, Chloe continued.

"In any case, like I was saying, we should not continue on this path. So, we need to take some measures. I propose that we should have a third party around us, especially when working late. We keep the door always open and not holding hands."

Femi responded with a resounded "Yes".

He was not in its entirety sure how that would work. One thing is sure; if Chloe settles on something to do, nobody can stop her. Not even him; Femi.

Over time, the strategy seemed to have worked. Chloe and Femi kept their raging emotions in the bag!

Lesson learnt! No more emotional dependence on anyone. With openness and sincerity, it can avert the greatest secret sin.

There was one thing she didn't want … to answer 'Yes' to a man for the wrong reasons, or at the wrong time.

An escape from Femi plagued her with the mystery of getting it right. She prayed,

*"Saviour, I am not good at it. My heart is fragile. Please, could you lead my relationships after your heart?"*

# FRIENDS WITHOUT BORDERS

*Anyone who withholds kindness from a
friend forsakes the fear of the Almighty.*

Chloe developed new relationships with others, alongside her great friendship with Femi.

Her mother encouraged this idea as a way of diverting her attention from Femi.

She soon got close to three other friends.

Supo, Tommy and Sheryl, were friends whom Chloe met in different, unexpected circumstances.

Supo was a good-looking secret admirer. Unknown to her, he had always been close by but concealed from view.

He had been watching her and how she committed herself to serve the Saviour. She loved singing, acting, serving, teaching, and counselling.

Chloe got involved in any activity to please the Redeemer. Supo enjoyed seeing others do it while he watched soundlessly.

During one meeting, they matched Supo and Chloe to pray for each other.

It was the first opportunity he had to exchange greetings with Chloe. After the service, they got together to talk more.

She soon noticed something reserved Supo. She took up the challenge to find out why someone who did not come across as quiet, would be so reserved.

Chloe saw a massive scar on the left side of his face. *"This could be a starting point,"* she thought.

One afternoon, Chloe took Supo by surprise. After exchanging greetings. They talked about events that had happened during the week. She raised her hands and touched his scar a little.

"What happened here?" she asked, staring dogmatically into his eyes. She noticed that Supo looked away immediately and felt uncomfortable. She added,

"I... I didn't mean to make you uncomfortable; if it makes you feel better, not telling me, please don't."

Deep inside, she was dying to know what the root of the scar on his face.

Minutes later, Supo broke the silence looking away from her as he spoke bit by bit.

"It's not that I don't want to discuss it; it hurts and brings back many memories; it broke my face."

Chloe has experienced what it means to have a scar. Knowing its effects, she smiled and said:

"Supo, I like you more because of the scar, and I would be a better friend to you."

She put her hands on his skin to cover the massive scar and said,

"You are more handsome now than you were before."
Supo turned to gaze at her, laughed and replied.

"You don't even know what I looked like before…"
Chloe interrupted him holding his chin resolutely.

"I don't; the way you look like now is more important to me than the way you looked before."
Supo lifted his hands on hers, saying,

"You are a good person, and I love your dimples."
His words were striking a chord in her heart. Chloe knew she was beginning another bond for life.

Supo told her everything as if he had to get everything off his chest before it's too late. From the accident that left him with the scar.

Due to his inability to continue his university education, he lost time while hospitalised. His disappointments and how he must start all over again - to Chloe, this was nothing new.

She, too, had never been to a higher institution. She felt it was a privilege to counsel Supo about trusting in the Saviour.

His promise of **"In His Time"** – was a hard message for her to follow sometimes. From then, their friendship began to flourish.

Amid their discussion, Chloe heard Tommy call out to her.

"Chloe! Chloe! We await your majesty to begin."

The drama practice was about to start. Chloe was one of the leaders in the team and from tip to toe involved in writing the scripts.

They needed her attention for an impending decision. Chloe replied,

"Guys, kindly start without me; I would be with you as soon as possible."

Tommy refused to move from his position until she took his request more imperative.

Supo pleaded with her to head forward with her meeting. Against her will, she hugged Supo and said "bye" to him.

As she walked away, she said to him,

"Remember, you are handsome".

Tommy tried to quiz her about Supo, and she smiled.

"Are you jealous?"

He responded stammering,

"Of w… ha… t?" Immediately he said it, and his eye started blinking.

"Don't know. Ask yourself! I can see you blink again. You know, anytime you blink, there is a lot more unspoken," she replied.

Tommy minimising eye contact walked past her, saying,

"Whatever!"

Chloe and Tommy were like 'Tom and Jerry'. At every opportunity, they had a go at each other; something Chloe enjoyed in their relationship.

She loved seeing others defeated from her teasing techniques. Tommy does not give up that easily; he loved getting back at her.

On occasions when someone else tried to get between them, both of them straight away turned the teasing on the individual.

Other friends knew and rarely interfered. Not until they had a field day of their friendly 'arguments'.

Tommy was a fun person to be with, and Chloe was always looking forward to meeting him.

He was handsome, relaxed and calm, and in his final year at the university.

Tommy was intelligent and a goal-getter; little wonder she loved to be around him.

He also had strong views about holiness and chastity, which is what the Saviour wants for all His children.

Knowing this was her goal and having struggled in her past, she felt in good company.

He would not take advantage of her. After all, she was a beloved sister. Was this true? Why then did he question Chloe's companions and discussions? Could there be anything more? She indomitable to find out.

Tommy walked over to her. He was slipping a note into her hands, as Chloe gave out her the final instructions for some actors.

*It would be the first time! Is he, in reality, apologising or offended?"*

Turning to question the content of the note, she saw him walking out of the building. Without opening it, Chloe made it snappy after him.

"Tom! Tom," she called, "Can we talk?"

Tommy turned chewing on pen and replied stylishness,

"Chloe, have you read the note?"

"Tom, why are you chewing your pen, shy again?" She teased him.

"I envisaged what I said still upset you," he commented, walking off.

"Wait!"

She unwrapped the note which read:

> *"Some of my university friends invited me to*
> *a concert tonight. Don't want to go alone!*
> *Would you mind joining me?*
> *Sorry for the short notice, Chatterbox!"*
>
> T.

Chloe looked up, exclaimed with a "huh!" trying to avoid Tommy flatters given by the unexpected invitation. She shouted out after him,

"Never knew I was this special!"

Tommy laughing, looking back with a glowing smile, replied,

"You are rather hot-headed! Chatterbox, I needed you to be talking to my friends."

Walking over to him, she replied,

"Nice, how much would you pay me? I know I am not special; we can make this for all intents and purposes, business!"

Tommy replied with a firm expression,

"In fact! Are you going with me or not? Or do you have any plan with the guy I saw with you? Were you robbing his face? Meh!"

"Now I know you are jealous," Chloe replied.
With an upset countenance, she declined the invitation.

"Are you this insensitive to other people's feelings? See you around."

She expressed her disapproval to his statement about Supo's scars.

Tommy rushed after her apologising for his verbal inadequacy. She turned around, smiled and replied,

"Apologies accepted, the invitation accepted. I would meet you are the concert" as she walked away, feeling asserted.

✿ ✿ ✿

The concert was fabulous. The stage lightings were glowing with different colours as the artists sang. One of the artists caught her admiration.

Her voice transcended all others, including Chloe's voice. She's never had as much goose pimples.

*"Mmh! The Saviour has them in different shades and kinds,"* she thought to herself.

Chloe resolved not to leave the venue without meeting the lady. Tommy sat in silence beside her as each of the artists sang.

He seems to enjoy himself as he watched her every move. She wondered what was going on in his mind. His friends were quiet.

She expected a group of loud friends with Tommy been the quiet one. The reserved was the case; Tommy seemed to do more talking.

*"Are his friends' nerds like him too? It was good to get to know his friends."*

*Like Mama Joe's words, "Show me your friends, and you tell me who you are."*

Tommy was a good reflection of his friends. They all dressed modestly with a conservative body and facial expressions.

Chloe excused herself after the concert and approached the artists backstage.

"Excuse me; I am Chloe. I could not help but compliment your talent before I leave. I sing too, but yours is way better than mine" she said giggling.

"Thank you," replied the lady with a confident smile.

"I am Sheryl, and I appreciate your compliments. It's all for His glory."

"I would like to know you better and learn from you. Especially how to hit those high notes."

Chloe persuaded her to create more time with her; with sparkling in her eyes.

Sheryl replied, "By all means."

A gentleman walked up to them. "Darling, that was fantastic as usual," reaching out for her hands.

"I know you!" Chloe exclaimed.

"You! You attend my church; you are rather quiet. I have never heard you speak before."

Chloe pointed to the gentleman.

Sheryl and her partner laughing together replied,

"Perfect description!"

"Nevertheless," he continued,

"I never knew someone was a silent admirer."

"My brother Joe knows you, both of you are one of a kind," she stated as the three of them laughed.

Sheryl's partner acknowledged her claims, describing how Joe and himself became acquainted.

"I was only telling Sheryl this minute I would like to be an acquaintance. Maybe a friend."

Chloe said as Tommy approached them.

"I am sorry, Tommy." Chloe walked toward him.

"I completely forgot you were with me. My pleasantries carried me away."

Moving her eyes from side to side, she continued,

"Tommy, meet Sheryl and her partner, Dave," Chloe uttered introducing everyone.

"I was complimenting her singing right now."

Tommy exchanged greetings with them. They exchange contacts and parted ways.

As they walked off, Tommy started laughing, acknowledging Chloe's habits.

"You are such a chatterbox! You can't help it straight away. You know, my friends had to leave because they could not wait any longer to say goodbye."

Chloe felt embarrassed by her lack of consideration for others. She pinched her lips with remorse.

"I am sorry. I completed forgot I was in the company of others."

Switching to her defensive tone, she continued,

"Remember, this was not a date. I am not special. It meant me filling a seat beside you. It doesn't matter if I don't say goodbye."

Tommy felt bewildered by her displaced defence and articulated confidence. He drew closer and took her hands, saying,

"Chloe, can I apologise once more for my attitude earlier today, forgive me."

Chloe's eyes were complimenting Tommy for his adulation towards her. She smiled with speechless acknowledgement. She received his apology by releasing her hands from his gentle grip.

They spent the rest of the evening together reminiscing about the concert. And how to modified some ideas into the drama scenes.

Chloe established a relationship with Sheryl. She was an interesting lady who was about ten years older than her.

Sheryl was not merely a talented singer; Sheryl was a great homemaker. She taught her how to marinate chicken and meat before cooking to produce tastier dishes.

Sheryl was a great interior decorator. She on her own merits decorated her home. The decorations ranged from the complementing curtains and sofa coverings to the handcrafted décor.

She made her own body and hair creams from the plants grown in her garden — a combination with natural ingredients.

Little wonder why her perms were exceedingly longer and firmer than other women. She wanted to avoid the chemicals used in commercial products for healthy living.

She seemed to have all the qualities needed in a wife. Chloe deliberated,

*"I have a long way to go and lots to learn if I have to be the wife, the Saviour wants me to be."*

Sheryl worked as a librarian in the African Culture Studies Department. A few yards from her accommodation.

Sheryl was a great friend to have, and she was ready to stick close to her new acquaintance.

# A NEW HORIZON

*The righteous choose their friends carefully,*
*but the way of the wicked leads them astray.*

Chloe finally got admission into the university. It's about five years after she finished secondary school.

Were her deep feelings of academic inadequacy now dealt with and long forgotten? The joy was indescribable.

*"Getting into the university; goal achieved,"* pictured Chloe.

She had to set the next goal, First Class perhaps. It would be ridiculous to stay at home for five years and then, end with a near failure.

She concluded that she would enjoy her relationships after the few bumps she had on the way.

Chloe switched on the 'Relationship Channel,' she has gained entrance into the university.

*"Was that going to be ideal or the most convenient position to take or am I setting up myself for failure?"*

Chloe questioned herself, knowing she was moving her goal post.

Chloe made another commitment to herself, driven by experiences.

*"I would get involved with school fellowship and less with church activities."*

Although she remained active in singles and drama leadership, she cut back other activities to enjoy being a student and her relationship with her Saviour in the new environment.

First, to make sure she made the right choices. Chloe had a chat with a church leader who had acted as a 'father'.

Ever since the relationship with her birth father, became dysfunctional.

The leader, pleased with her decisions, reminded her he did the same when he was in the university.

He noted, he did not balance his 'faith commitments' with his schoolwork. He encouraged Chloe to balance things.

He admonished her that the priority should be her academics. They talked about the musical mission band of the campus fellowship.

The church leader explained how he was a member of the musical group, during his university days. In his opinion, it seemed a good starting point for Chloe.

Somehow, it was better going to university as a mature person. It gave Chloe a better perspective of who she was, what she wanted, and what she was aiming for in future.

Chloe knew she was still a novice, on choices of men. An area she had not dealt with, beyond a shadow of a doubt since childhood.

Meeting new people during orientation week was a welcome activity.

Chloe loved meeting people, albeit, she was not keen on keeping long-term friendships any more.

The second day during registration, the sun was scorching hot. She was so tired and frustrated with the admission process.

Chloe was seeking shade from the heat of the sun when a young man bumped into her.

"Hey, man! Look where you are going," Chloe yelled out in an upset tone.

"My sincere apologies" was his quick response.

"I am Remi. I know you are Chloe. Nice to meet you."
Flattered but still with a stern face, Chloe asked,

"How do I know you? Where did you find out my name? Who are you? Are you a stalker?"

Remi responded to her questions with a beautiful smile as she watched his beard glow in the sun.

Chloe could not help but respond with a smile.
Now relaxed, she continued.

"Could you kindly answer my questions, gentleman?"

"That is honourable to call me a gentleman, my lady," Remi answered in a tender tone.

Chloe blushing whispered,

"All right! Don't bother. I would see you around," as she walked away.

"Hey, Chloe! Wait up. If truth be told, don't you want your answers?"
Chloe grinned.

"Don't you want to tell me?"

Remi chuckled.

"I mull over the fact that we would make a good match."

"Haha! In your world! Don't flatter yourself. I am leaving for my department. Are you heading my way? I bet you know my department too!"

Remi ushered her to take the first step, and he said,

"You are right again. You are in Sociology, and I am in Economics."

"Interesting", Chloe sighed, clearing her throat.

"How old am I? Where do I come from, where?

Remi interrupted.

"I am not a soothsayer."

With a plain looked he carried on,

"The information I know about you, I found out yesterday and this morning."

Chloe looked puzzled, awaiting a further explanation for his knowledge of her.

He continued, "I was standing beside you at the administration office yesterday morning. I heard your name announced. Rather than responding, you said, 'Thank you, Saviour,' and a quiet prayer before answering."

Smiling Chloe added,

"Really?"

"It assured me you had had an encounter with the Saviour. I have met with him too. I would love to be your friend. Please tell me I am not wrong?"

Chloe paused without a sound, listened with her head bowed a tad and nodded.

She thought,

*"Saviour, thank you! I was in a good mood. Only imagine if I had the anger suit on her! Thank you for giving me a new friend."*

She felt assured that the Saviour had meant this to be. Chloe, now comfortable replied,

"Thank you for your words; you are very kind. It's me; no denial again. Did you bump into me by design?"

Remi mystified replied,

"Noooo! Fair, can we say that is the way the Saviour wanted us to meet?"

"You are right!" Chloe beamed.

Remi called out, "I am starving," as they walked past the Student Union building.

"Do you mind having lunch with me," he asked with a thoughtful tone.

Chloe surprised said, "Wait, wait! How many ladies have you asked out for lunch? Is this a date?

In defence, baffled Remi answered, "Not at all. It's an innocent request. Don't worry. I am not on campus to pay for ladies' lunches."

Laughing at the top of her voice, Chloe said,

"Kidding. I can walk you there. I must leave because I have a friend waiting for me in the department...

A male friend!" Remi chuckled and said,

"No pressure, Chloe. It's a free world," walking her into the building.

✿ ✿ ✿

After that lovely encounter with Remi, they kept in touch enjoying each other's company.

She headed to the department for an appointment with Ben. Chloe took it all in her stride.

The week soon rolled into lecture periods. One friendship Chloe did not need to make afresh was with Ben.

Ben was one of her old friends from church, a final year student in her department.

Having a familiar face around was the best way to start university. Chloe perceived him as a big brother.

Admitting she couldn't deny flashes of thoughts that *"whoever marries him would be a lucky woman."*
Ben was tall, slim, and handsome. He was also a mixed-race, a unique feature that was not popular in Chloe's environment.

Like her, Ben had not found life funny, but through his difficulties, he had held on strong.

*"Am I getting attracted to him?"* Chloe asked herself after a few months of being in school.

All along, she knew he was charming and funny; she enjoyed his company. But, why is Chloe always getting attracted to men that have had a difficult life? Or those from an apparent humble background?

Even though she could not define her experience as ordinary, life has a way of redefining people.

Chloe continued to develop a positive relationship with Ben. She did, without letting her feelings get in the way.

Again, there was a goal; he would leave university soon. He would be an excellent mentor to have.

Once he's gone, that would be it; she encouraged herself. The real question she had never addressed was,

"Does Ben have any ideas about her flowing through, on his mind?"

Ben was one of the student leaders in the department, who organised the departmental excursion to Ghana.

It was a dream come true! Chloe had always dreamt of travelling out of the shores of her country.

It was a perfect idea; she thought as the day approached. She could observe Ben more, know the person he is.

If possible, appreciate him more…

*"I am daydreaming,"* she smiled to herself.

Approaching him on the hallway, she yelled out,

"Ben, the trip to Ghana, is a dream come true."

Ben turned around, looking at her with good cheer.

"I am looking forward to it too. Have you signed up yet?"

"Not yet, would do once I am ready. I want to clear up some expenses first."

"If you need any help, let me know. How are Mama Joe and Joe? I have not seen them recently."

Still excited, she replied,

"They are good! Not been home for two weeks, though."

"Chloe, you have changed so much. I remember the first time I met you with Joe. You were such a shy little one. I can't seem to reconcile how you have changed so much."

Chloe pinching her lips, replied,

"I know, right! Life brings the best out of you!"

"It sure does, Ghana would be fun, I promise!" he replied.

"I have confidence in you" feeling a sense of assurance as if Joe was speaking to a different her.

Ben had always treated her like a child.

"That was the way he made her feel when she was around him."

❈ ❈ ❈

Two months later, the group was on a road trip to Ghana.

The journey would take them through the Benin Republic and Togo route. After about five hours, their bus arrived Cotonou at about two-thirty-five pm.

They drove through the toll station to confirm their legal documents.

The coach steered into the central market, a boundary between Nigeria and the Benin Republic.

The scenery was busy with selling and buying, rain or sunshine; some hawkers could be seen pushing their products down the potential buyers' throats.

The snacks and goods were quite cheaper than in Nigeria. She now understood why many traders trade with Cotonou.

Most of her companions were out and about checking out the scenery.

Chloe sat in the coach as though she would be a victim of kidnapping if she stepped out.

When everyone was told to visit the toilet before leaving, she only attempted to step out.

Funny enough, Ben spoke a few words with her; he was with his friends all the time.

An hour later, everyone arrived back on the coach to begin their drive to Lome, Togo.

It took about three hours. Most of the students slept after filling up their hunger stomachs.

The journey was getting exhausting. Although Chloe loved the scenery, she was longing for her close friends.

Is Ben not going to pay any attention to her? His image flooded her mind when she dozed off.

It was a whistle from the border police officer that woke her up. It was time for another checking point.

The Togo border seemed stricter than the Benin Republic. The officers spoke in French; they looked terrifying.

In fact! They delayed their entry for another hour before their clearance.

The border officers refused to believe the information provided to them by the travellers.

They had to call the Nigerian officers and university to confirm the reasons for their travel.

Chloe tried to check with Ben; what was going on. He seemed to ignore her again.

*"This is not the picture I had about this journey"* she sighed in regret.

"Such a group of sad people!" One student exclaimed. Everyone pushed into the verge of acute alertness.

"In fact!" responded another.

"These border officers wasted our time."

Another continued,

"Do you know they occupy their country with a bunch of lazy folks?"

"Why would you describe a country like that?" challenged the next.

"I have facts," he responded with an accent.

"What facts?" Two or more replied as they interrupted him.

"The whole country spends its afternoon having an obligatory siesta. That include schools and all government officials. They worship their president like a god," he continued.

"Why would they do that? Sound dumb to me." Someone responded to the educated informant.

"All I know the whole country does, it's historical, traced to their colonial masters." He responded.

Their arguments continued on and on. It was a breath of fresh air.

The topic created a heated debate on slavery, colonial and its effect on the African continent.

Chloe's mind wondered about sleeping every afternoon. How interesting will that be? But the whole country? Seems like a bad idea!

For the next three hours, the gist went from one topic to another. They cracked several jokes for the pleasures of all the travellers.

Chloe felt at home; At last, she took part in the discussions. It was fun until someone shouted through the dark traffic lights.

"We are in Accra," with a sense of attainment

"Yes, we are in" echoed another.

"Wait, we are stopping at a traffic light. What! Stopping at the traffic does not happen in Ibadan?" Chloe exclaimed.

"Haha! Not in your wildest dream," someone replied her.

The next traffic light and the third was the same. The drivers observe traffic light regulations in Accra, Ghana.

How I wish it were the same where we were coming from - Nigeria. Or Ibadan where she was born and lived all her life.

She picked up her journal and wrote her latest observations.

Quarter to eleven pm, they drove into the University of Ghana campus. It was a great relieve that the leaders arranged the visitors unit.

They were all lodged in the Legon Hall student accommodation.

They settled in for the night after the eventful journey.

The next morning just as the sun rose, everyone got ready. Each individual sorted out breakfast.

Chloe sought the cheapest option, which not an ideal, a small portion of bread and a cup of tea.

She could not afford to misuse the little funds she had. The day's travel around the city started at about nine in the morning.

They visited the Akosombo dam and the waterfalls. The gold mine, and other attractions.

Everyone took pictures and reached out to meet new people. Chloe loved the people of Accra.

In her opinion, the impression she has about the people are that they seemed to be better law-abiding than Nigeria.

The streets were clean, and all the transport facilities were in good order.

The taxies on the road were all in excellent conditions. Chloe's most considerable amusement was that Ben had only spoken a few words to her.

The next day they visited some university faculties. They met with students from a similar department and spent the day together.

Not too long, William (Will for short) a student from the host university started flirting with her.

"Hey! Would you like to go out with me later for drinks?"

William asked out of the blue, while they prepared the departmental debate. It was evident to the whole group.

"Was that meant for me?" Chloe asked herself, checking around.

*"I am the closest to him. Meaning the target of the question is me."*

To her, it was an embarrassment! She smiled and said,

"Can we talk about it later?"

*"Can't I be invisible anywhere I go without desirability,"* she asked herself.

She ended up declined the drink offer. Williams exchanged contact information with Chloe, with a promise to visit her in Nigeria.

Chloe was sweet and polite throughout the encounter with Will.

She knew that was the last day she would ever set her eyes on him.

The contact with Williams seemed to have made Ben uncomfortable.

She observed a slight withdrawal from him for the rest of the evening. Chloe felt a bit unsettled by what he was going through.

She would not allow it to cross the emotional boundaries with him.

Ben's friends started teasing him to change the idea he had about Chloe. She watched from a distance, as they taunted him.

"Rather, the 'sister idea' he had should be adapted to his 'woman idea'."

He denied it at all points; It was apparent he had 'the' impression all along too.

Chloe did not allow his tossing positions to affect her. If he turned around to ask her for a date, she might disappoint him.

She was not ready to lose another friend, to the complexities of relationships.

She wanted to savour every bit of time she had left with him, with a pleasant memory. Things should not be messed up.

## ❀ ❀ ❀

The rest of the trip, little by little, became quiet. Chloe got the message:

Ben was saying, *"I don't want you to be around me."*

His withdrawal became more evident; after the visit to Ghana.

She got busier with her coursework. The distance between them in due course created a void.

Ben left the university after his graduation. There was little or no communication between them.

Chloe was proud of herself; no hurt and could handle her emotions better. Chloe suppressed her unfulfilled experiences and memories with someone around the corner.

She seemed to have formed the habit of not dealing with relationships out and out.

All along, Mife was a secret admirer or stalker. Chloe often passed him on her way from church.

She soon discovered they were both in the same faculty, although different departments.

He was a postgraduate student. From a distance, he was shy and quiet, a man of few words till you get to know him.

Her encounter with Mife started with a meeting on the bus on her way back from church. He introduced himself uninterrupted, although she could hardly hear him.

Chloe assumed it was the first time they had met. He knew her, however, from a distance for at least a year earlier.

The first encounter was as simple as expected. Soon, Mife was tutoring one of her elective courses from his department.

To begin with, she avoided anything to do with him because he seemed too shy for her. Nevertheless, Tobi, one of Chloe's girlfriend, was already friends with him.

Mife and Tobi were both in the political science department, which made it tricky for her to avoid him.

The relationship soon went beyond the department. Tobi persuaded her to visit his room with her and Mife started visiting her.

She was unsettled about him all the same.

# WELCOMED DISTRACTION

*The wisdom of the prudent is to*
*give thought to their ways.*

The Student Union has started again. "It's not a rumour,"

Chloe thought. Months into her studies, as she was adjusting to her new routine, trouble erupted.

They had boycotted lectures; students were outside rioting. Could it be about welfare on campus, particularly students' accommodation?

She was glad when she moved out of the student housing when she did. She could not stand the over-crowdedness.

In the past, at least once every year, there is a student demonstration on the campus.

It would lead to shut down activities on campus until further notice. Chloe made enquired from the BQ mates.

It was another face-off; between the Independent Student Electoral Commission (ISEC) and the University authorities.

According to her mates, the student union executive conducted an election.

Nevertheless, when the new officers got sworn in, proper procedures were ignored. This development created a legal tussle which exploded into a major crisis.

Chloe was itching for more details. She rushed into the bath. She was thinking about her friends living in student accommodations.

Chloe's heart increased with a heavy breath created by a wedge of deep fear.

She filled her mind with the flash images of Remi, Chuks, Tobi and all her friends.

She rushed out again, headed to her room to make a few calls, to make sure they were alright. Remi picked at the first ring,

"Are you alright? What's happening there? Do you want me to come over? Have you eaten?"

"Chloe! Chloe, can I answer the question or questions now. Your call woke me up. I am alright. Things are tense here, and I would not recommend that you come over my accommodation."

"Why? I would be alright; I can take care of myself," she protested.

"I know, but I would get dressed and would be with you shortly. Lastly, I have eaten, have I answered all your questions."

"Yes, you have," she replied, but with heavy breathing, accompanied by a racing pulse.

*"Why am I getting pulses, it's Remi, Remi, my brother!"* Scolding herself

Next was Chuks; he gave similar responses as Remi; he would come over to hers too.

By the time she called the sixth friend, they were all coming over.

Chloe took a quick bath, begun preparation for a meal to feed the empty bellies coming.

Seyi showed up first because his accommodation was closest to hers. He confirmed that the university authorities disapproved of the election.

As a Consequence, swearing-in was an act of gross misconduct.

In fact! Seyi heard they expelled the student union president, leading to the peak of the crisis.

Remi and Chuks showed up at the same time, running in as if a ghost chased them in.

In a panic, Chloe jumped; leapt over the edge of the bed, blinking her eyes in fear. She reached out to her pillow and held it across her chest.

They burst into laughter at the sight of the alarm she was in; together, they echoed.

"We were joking. We planned to run in a few yards away. Don't you know your room is in the residential area?"

"So, you frightened me!" She protested, again and again, stamping her feet on the spring bearing bed.

The three men kept laughing together on this rear occasion. They got Chloe to express her fearful weakness.

"I never knew you could be afraid, iron lady!" Seyi voiced out, pulling the pillow away from her hands.

Wearing an emotional face, Chloe responded,

"I am not an iron lady. I care, worry and want to make sure my friends were alright. Guess, the reason I called you all this morning. Even though no one cared to call me."

She used the pillow to start a pillow fight with the boys.

"You have a point," Remi echoed, taking his seat by her reading table.

"We are sorry, caring friend" Chuks stuttered.

"Speak for yourself," Seyi concluded.

"Chloe enjoys teasing others; she should eat a slide of her baked cake sometimes," he said in amusement.

"What do you mean?" Chloe giggled. She resumed the pillow fight with Seyi, a knock on the door disrupted them.

"That must be Tobi," she said as she headed for the door. She lifted the curtains to find Tobi with two other friends.

"Tobi, you looked exhausted. Are you okay?" Her first expression as she opened the door.

"I am not okay; we ran half of the way here. The whole campus is in pandemonium."

"The news spreading is that students should leave the campus for their safety," Remi added as they welcomed Tobi and her friends.

Chuks interrupted, "The ISEC had accused the university authorities of interfering."

"Interfering in what?" questioned Chloe.

"In the affairs of the students' union elections. In protest, they started the riot, but the authorities were adamant."

Chloe listened as each of her friends narrated their versions of the events on campus.

According to Remi, the face-off took a new dimension in court. Therefore, the university authorities dissolved the latest elected student union government.

"I heard there were at least forty-two student union leaders suspended."

"Are you sure, CNN Tobi?" Remi queried her rumour.

"Yes," one of the ladies with Tobi responded.

"My brother is one of the executive members. He alleged the authorities planned to introduce an increase to the tuition fees."

"What!" Chloe exclaimed.

"The student union thinks the university is interfering with the election. To distract the union from the planned new fees, the authority aimed at disrupting the elections. The aim is to silence all the voices that would attempt to disrupt their plans."

Tobi's friend concluded

"But is forty-two students not too much?" Chloe asked with stooped shoulders.

"Why is the university playing politics with people's lives? I pray it would not affect the academic year," Seyi echoed.

"Sure, it has disrupted the semester examinations already," Remi chipped in.

They continued to talk about all the happenings on campus. They discussed how demonstrators are burning tyres and vandalising properties.

They spoke of the numbers of lives lost in the previous riots. They feared any intervention from the military and the federal government.

"If the university gets shut down by the federal government, it would be indefinite," Seyi weighed in,

"Don't be pessimistic!" Chloe echoed, pacing around the room.

"Relax, Chloe, it means a break," Chuks threw in smiling. "I miss home."

"Mummy's boy! Not for me. I prayed to the Saviour before I started university. My plead was that I would study for four years. I am hoping for the best outcome."

"Why don't we talk to the Saviour about it rather than allowing fear overcoming us," Remi concluded.

Each expressed their concerns to the Saviour.

They resolved that for their safety, they would head to their homes.

Chloe knew this was home for her and wished all her friends well as they parted.

Chloe took a walk to the centre of the conflict.

Taking a route around the staff residential area, she approached the battlefield.

From a distance she watched the angry students chanting.

"We no go, gree oo! We no go, gree! Hear our shouting! We no go. gree!"

The leaders shouted the "Aluta continua!"

Others replied "vitória é certa."

Meaning "The struggle continues, victory is certain."

The thick smoke and flames from the burning tires and cars covered the whole atmosphere. Breathing became a ticking time bomb.

After fifteen minutes of watching the horrible scene, Chloe heard the emergency armed mobile officers approaching the gates of the campus.

The confrontation degenerated into a stand-off between the army and the protesting students.

They threw tear gases to disperse the students. But things worsen. The police made several more arrests.

She gave up the watch and returned to her room to talk to the Saviour, about the whole mess on campus.

The situation would soon become unbearable. Many of the students had already left the university campus.

Before Chloe gained admission, students were on strike. The university calendar was in complete disarray.

Chloe prayed she would complete her degree within the regular academic four years. But with an attack arising, her faith seemed shaken.

Later that evening, the authority announced the shutdown of school until further notice.

It was hopeless! Chloe had to plan something to do while they shut the university. By this time, all her friends had left the campus.

She approached Mr Eze, the owner of the IT establishment, whose office was opposite the main university gate.

She took courses on introductory IT and Microsoft packages. He was glad to support her and other students.

They found his establishment as a place to gain new skills to keep themselves busy. Chloe met new people in the office, one of whom was Fletcher.

✿ ✿ ✿

Fletcher was not attractive at first sight, but he was brilliant, everyone in the office knew that. They called him to sort out most queries.

And the one left in charge of the office whenever Mr Eze was inaccessible. As the weeks went by, workers started whispering about Fletcher's undue attention to Chloe.

"Could this be true," Chloe asked herself.

Chloe refused to see the writing on the wall until Fletcher asked for her photograph. Staring emotionless at him, she pondered,

"That was audacious of him in front of everyone." Feeling so embarrassed, she muttered,

"What do you need my picture for?"

She was not one to act loose in front of people or fall without difficulty for a flirt asking for her picture. Immediately, she refused.

A week later, Fletcher in public told her he had always watched her sing in the choir.

He said, "You sing like an angel."

Chloe froze. Another secret admirer? Not for now?.

She responded emotionless with a verbal denial of self-worthiness.

"I know nothing new about my voice." She avoided any facial contact with him.

Fletcher realising, he would not get Chloe to have a conversation with him, said:

"I attend your church; you can find out."

He stepped out of the classroom to avoid further embarrassment. Immediately he left, Chloe turned to one of the girls,

"Is it true, have you seen that guy in church before?"

"He is not that guy. His name is Fletcher. Yes, he attends our church."

She responded in sharp contrast, looking away.

"Can you see you embarrassed him? He hardly speaks, he did today, and you drove him away. A simple compliment about your voice you couldn't handle it."

Chloe was uncomfortable and judged because she was not expecting such an outburst.

She walked out of the building at a fast pace, called Femi to find out about him. It turned out to be true.

Fletcher was the younger brother of one of the church members.

Although she seldom spoke to her, she knew she was one of the leaders.

Fletcher attended the church whenever he was in town or during breaks from his university. Chloe felt a mix of awkwardness and infuriation.

"I am not interested in another saga now," she thought as her face exploded in anger.

Though she tried to find out how much he knew about her, she was getting irritated.

She was not willing to talk too long because Fletcher was the last guy; she wanted to have anything to do with at the moment.

She asked him firmly,

"Why do you need my photograph?"

He replied in terror, looking at the computer screen.

"I want to draw a picture of you."

Feeling ever more embarrassed that she had been too harsh on him, she responded:

"Are you an artist too?"

Fletcher told her he could draw, and that he often makes portraits for fun.

To Chloe, it was nothing new because her brother, Joe, was also an artist. Then, playing the 'drawing your picture' card would not work.

Chloe discussed with her mother. She advised,

"Whatever his reasons, Chloe, give him the picture. I would pray with you".

Mama Joe suggested that she should complete her training uninterrupted. Whatever it would cost her.

The next day, she gave him the photograph, but she was not looking forward to seeing or collecting a drawing.

What exactly could be going on in his head? What is she going to do about men getting attracted to her, especially when she has not asked for it? She remembered what her primary school teacher said.

"It would interest no one to have you."

Her teeth had attracted many to her. But not of necessity the men she dreamt of as 'Prince Charming'.

The question remains, what does the Saviour say about it all? Without explanation, the feeling she had was, why Fletcher?

## FRIENDS LIKE BROTHERS

*A friend loves at all times, and*
*a brother is born for a time of adversity.*

Chloe has indeed had many male friends, but what she long for were friends like her brothers. Long-term friends with agape love.

There were a few men she would refer to as friends closer than brothers.

Many faded away after her university degree. Seyi was one of Chloe's friends from the church; he had been in most of the youth activities with her.

As luck would have it, he had never broken her trust in him. He was someone she could count on to support her.

There were a few things about him that were quite annoying. He talked too much and repeated whatever he had already said.

A habit most people would find frustrating. As a good friend, she came to accept him the way he was; over time, she got used to him.

Even as friends, they shared leadership roles in the church's drama team. Often, they would discuss scriptwriting.

But, foremost, Chloe focused on the welfare of the group, while Seyi handled the direction of their plays. Most of their practices were usually night vigils once a month.

She filled the group's favourite time with loads of snacks and teasing sessions. It was not surprising that she met others' needs with her hospitality gifts.

Chloe and Seyi made a great team. She felt she could run her ideas past him. She was often safe with the decision they came up with together.

Seyi was a great listener. Chloe remembered when she made her first decision about where to fellowship.

She concluded, she would have to remain in her local church. Because of her ongoing commitments. Especially with the drama group and the need to join the student fellowship on campus.

Chloe encountered some resistance from some church members.

They accused her of backsliding from her faith. It was a difficult time for her, but Seyi stood by her and urged her to follow her heart.

He agreed he would have taken a similar step when he gained admission into the university.

Seyi every so often visited Chloe's room. Like Mama Joe, she had turned out to be a great cook; entertaining people was one of her hobbies. Chloe and Seyi became a support system for each other on campus.

They shared advice and opinions on life and relationships. Can anything ever go wrong with this friendship?

Once Seyi finished lectures, he headed straight to Chloe's room. He has his mindset on for his favourite meal of black-eyed beans.

Not only was her place, the feeding headquarters, but her room was also his napping joint. Chloe's accommodation became a refreshing hub for most of her friends.

✿ ✿ ✿

There was also Chuks, Chloe's brother from another mother. He was such a sweetheart to the core.

He was tall and handsome with a soft feminine voice, like that of an angel. In reality, that was the first quality that attracted Chloe to him.

She met him during the fellowship mission, the musical band audition.

Even though the group's test was taking forever, immediately Chuks started singing, there was complete silence in the room.

That was when she told herself,

*"He is a keeper. Without a doubt, I would make friends with him."*

After the audition, Chuks walked her back to her room. And that was the beginning of a lifelong agape love friendship.

Her friendship with Chuks was another one that was confusing to others from the outside.

Only those close to them knew they were no more than good friends. Both were photogenic and taking pictures became a fun activity; they enjoyed together.

Chloe and Chuks would sing duets along with their circle of friends.

Singing with him was like heaven as they harmonised with each other voice. Sometimes, she wondered if she could break her promise.

*"Should I fall recklessly in love with him?* "

It was hard. Chloe daily guarded her frame of mind for Chuks. But she also maintained purity while speaking to the Saviour about him.

On one occasion, Chloe attended a wedding with Chuks. The comments buzzing their ears were,

"You guys are a perfect couple."

The remarks brought blushes and smiles each time she heard it. It didn't stop her from thinking whether they would ever be 'perfect couple.'

She fantasised, walking down the aisle with Chuks by her side. It was an undeniable fact; she would not ask him to marry her.

If ever he would the question, she was ready to give a 'Yes.' Other times, she wondered if her mind was not playing tricks on her.

*"Our ways are not God's ways,"* she reflected deflecting her plaguing thoughts. Chloe encouraged herself and trusted Him for her future.

Chloe took her friends to visit her mother for hot meals, which they needed as students after a hard day's work.

Mama Joe acquainted herself with Chloe for her choices of friends. Mama Joe expressed in polite observations.

"You are 23 years old. Your friendships lack close female companions as expected."

To Chloe, it was a mere reflection of her experience with girls from her childhood involvements.

The first time she met with Chuks family came with mixed feelings.

Although it was an opportunity to meet them, she was sad because of the circumstances.

Chuks lost his father a few months into their first year in the university. Besides, he had been going through tough times in his studies.

He needed all the support she could give him, but no one could comfort as a mother would.

It was a hard, rough journey to his home; his mother was glad he visited with his friends. His parent's church led the way-keeping service.

The crowd cried as they narrated their memories. The impacts Chuks' father had on their lives.

Chloe reflected on her life, wondering what people would say of her after she dies.

Chloe walked over to Chuks and his other friends, after the service. The group of friends kept him company for the rest of the evening.

The impact of life after death was a reflective moment. She renewed her determination to reach out to others. It was the primary goal of her existence.

✿ ✿ ✿

Remi was another of Chloe's cherished relationship on campus. Reflecting on her first encounter with him always fills her heart with joy.

*"Talk about the redeemer ordering their steps."*

He was the super attractive young man she had spotted during the orientation week. They got talking and exchanged details.

Each morning they met, walking together and discovering the campus. Thus, a close bond formed. He was in the same department as Tobi (Mife's friend).

Remi was a down-to-earth guy focusing on integrity, purity and love for the Saviour. Qualities which he shared with Chloe.

She knew he was God-sent to her to walk on the journey for the next four years.

Chloe decided not to have any funny ideas about him; even though he was attractive, intelligent, witty and good-looking.

Chloe felt the need to have an open discussion about their feelings. She longed to know how it would affect the relationship with the Redeemer.

One afternoon after class, Remi waited for her at the departmental square. Chloe's heart skipped in beats watching him read from a distance.

*"Remi is a handsome creature. I bet the Saviour took out some time to complete His work on him."*

Walking towards him, he lifted his eyes and smiled.

"Chlo, you know I saw you from a distance. Why were you staring?"

"Nothing," she responded on the spur of the moment, pinching her lips.

"What's wrong with staring at you?"

"Are you not good enough to attract attention? An attraction from this beautiful damsel."

Remi's face flushed with his adoring smile, said

"Yes, my dear, you are right! I would never forget the day I met you forever."

"I share the same sentiment." Both joked recounting the events of the day.

"Rem"

"Yes, ma," Remi replied.

"What do you want from me? Can we define what we are?"

Chloe fiddled with her feet as a great sense of unease flood her brow.

Remi, relaxed as his usual, looked up, adjusting the notebooks on his lap.

"I have been expecting this moment. I know you too well now. You are direct and firm. I appreciate these qualities in you."

"I know, Rems', let's talk about us."

"I am getting there."

"Sorry, I interrupted." Chloe reached out her hands to cover his.

"I want us to be friends. I need a friend who can be honest and blunt with me…"

As Remi shared his desire for their relationship, Chloe's mind wandered a mile away.

"Looks like I would remain in the friendship zone for a long time." Her thoughts interrupted by his voice.

"Chlo, Chlo, did you hear anything I said? Are you alright?"

"Yes, I did, I felt the need for the clarification so that we can create boundaries…"

Chloe continued in a fit of religious mannerism. She once again put aside her need to have someone more than a friend.

*"Pleasing the Saviour requires everything, even a desire for Rems'."*

She scrutinised to herself.

*"But does He not want me to be happy or be with someone like Remi?"*

She questioned His thoughts towards her.

Remi continued.

"I aim to please the Saviour; I understand that's your aim too. I would not miss my words. If anything impedes our aim, we agree to end this friendship."

Chloe's heart torn apart; on the one hand, she wished she never asked.

On the other, she was glad they created boundaries.

They both agreed they would remain friends that are closer than brothers.

Remi would be a 'brother', Chloe said to herself. It was tempting to experiment with 'something' more than a brother.

But she with no trouble overcoming her imaginations with the fact that he, Remi was younger than she.

Those days, being younger than a lady, in cultural terms, was unacceptable. It was against the social norm for relationships.

Chloe loved Remi too much to let go. She would save him the torment of considering her, as someone more than a sister.

Yet, it was hard to know how he felt for her. By the second year, their circle of friends increased. But, this never diminished their closeness, because they have agreed to be friends.

They kept their agreement of the purity of their relationship. Remi and Chloe's decision served a selfish purpose.

It drew wrongful attention away from them because there was a general assumption; both were a couple — especially those with wrong motives getting attracted to them.

Remi and Chloe read, walked, and ate together. They visited each other and nicknamed as the faculty 'bonhomie or buddy'.

Alongside another friend, Kunle, they started a prayer group. They discussed with the Saviour about their future.

Such a sweet moment! If either of them were not in the fellowship, people would question the other party.

They treated them as a 'caretaker' to the other. Others seemed jealous accusing Chloe of denying them the opportunity to go out with Remi.

There was nothing more than 'Agape love' between them.

Some guys, trying to get close to Chloe also accused Remi of the same thing. There were times they would walk from their faculty to Chloe's room.

They would spend the rest of the evening together. Chloe would walk to Remi's student accommodation.

They relished each other's company, sometimes holding hands under the shining stars.

Remi would do the same and escort her back to her room with the pretence that he wanted to keep her safe.

A walk that would last over an hour most times; nevertheless, they both knew he was fond of her company.

Whenever Chloe visited his student accommodation, some boys would start yelling,

"Remi! Remi! Your wife is here".

Although it became embarrassing, she knew they meant no harm. They knew her well enough.

If Remi was not available, there were self-appointed announcers all around the block. They shouted as she approached.

"He is not around; we would let him know you visited." Remi and Chloe adapted and appreciated the comments.

Toward the second year, Remi's sister was getting married.

Remi invited Chloe to travel with him. Admitting, she was excited about going to a 'party.' The question on her mind was,

"As what to him?"

Chloe knew deep down within her that Remi was a friend, but how would his family perceive her?

Her impression on others was an overrated burden to her, which sometimes affected Chloe's decisions.

Chloe felt confused and afraid to express these fears to Remi. She was not ready to plant any seeds of doubt on the landscape of their emerging friendship — a sign of insecurity and fear of rejection — a haunting shadow of the past.

Some of his family members already knew her, so she would not be a total stranger. Remi's sister and brother had visited the campus a few times.

She was confident they were alright with her Platonic friendship with their brother. Her anxiety was his father.

She could not handle another rejection from Remi's father on the dot, as her father did.

Chloe still had a longing for a father figure in life, despite being in her twenties.

*"But this was not the time to dwell on the past,"* she thought.

Remi and Chloe were absent on Friday during the engagement.

They had an examination at the university. First thing on Saturday morning, they were at the bus park where they boarded a bus to Ile-Ife.

The journey was quiet; He seemed he had a lot on his mind. Remi distracted himself with his reading.

Chloe enjoyed music on her 'Walkman' player. She sat close to the window, enjoying the scenery and the interactions of passers-by while the driver drove on.

On arrival in their home, they welcomed her with enthusiasm. Remi introduced her to the rest of his family as a friend from university.

She felt uncomfortable pinching her nails, to distract from the rising tension within.

There was an assumption that by bringing a lady for a family occasion, the couple had crossed a line of commitment.

Consequently, it is something more than brotherliness or friendship between them.

It was Remi's mother's attitude that shocked her. Despite the fact, she welcomed Chloe with eagerness into her home.

Several questions that followed in quick succession overwhelmed her.

"When did you start befriending my son?"
She asked Chloe, unguarded as fear came rushing into her spine. She continued:

"Do you know he is my first son and the next head of this family?"

Chloe readjusted her sitting position to respond, but she carried on,

"What state did you say you are from?"
Chloe's, who had lost the ability to answer the first two questions, replied with, "Bendel State."

The look on her face was expressive, and grave silence followed afterwards.

*"Meenn! This woman is better in the sudden questioning game than I am. Is this how I make people feel? Not good!"* she thought as she tried to keep composed in the silence.

Chloe was glad Remi had to run an errand for his father. So, she had spared him the embarrassing questions his mother had asked her.

Chloe knew immediately; Remi's mother was not ready for her son to go out with someone outside their tribe.

She was sure, Remi's mother had already articulated her position and opposition to any idea of Remi's future wife.

They both stared in front of the TV screen in silence. Moments later, his mother stood up to welcome other family members, coming in for the wedding in a few hours.

*"This is a welcomed break."*

Chloe reassured herself. Although exhausted, she was glad she did not ask for her age.

Remi's mother would have been so distressed to find out she was older than her son!

Pondering over her experience with Remi's mother, Chloe concluded about Remi. He would never make a move to cross over the lines of emotional attraction with her.

She toyed with the idea that he might...

*"What if Remi pursues me and fights for me disregarding his mother's views? It wouldn't be a bad idea. He is a dear friend. What greater blessing is there than to marry a friend!"*

After the wedding, Chloe headed back to school by herself. Remi had to stay behind to spend time with his family.

While Remi was away for the next week, she enjoyed the company of Chuks.

The truth remains, as far as Chloe's heart's conviction; "Remi was a friend."

Somewhere in the world, there is another Remi that tick all the boxes for her.

# POOR DECISIONS HURTS

*Choose for yourselves this day,*
*whom you will serve.*

Chloe had settled into her new life as a single lady living away from her family for the first time.

She loved it.

Chloe remembered her discussion her need for privacy with Mama Joe.

"Mamma mia!" she called Mama Joe in jest, walking home from class.

"Hello! Hello. You sound happy!" Mama Joe replied, expecting her next words.

"Mama, I want to get my place."

Mama laughed and replied,

"It's about time. I have been looking forward to this independence."

"Mama, I imagined…"

"If you ask me, it is a good decision, and I support you altogether. Make sure you keep in touch."

Chloe surprised, replied,

"Mama, are you tired of me? I am not moving out right now."

"No, not at all, Chloe. I am waiting for you. Get home soon. You have some errands to run for me." Mama Joe added giggling.

"Okay mama, on my way."

*"Can a mother be more supportive than this?"*

Chloe smiled, thanking the Saviour for her wonderful mother.

Her new accommodation was one room in a rectangular boys' quarters (BQ) compound behind her professor's house.

There was an entrance in front, leading to a car park.
There was no fence behind the living apartment but a path that led to her department.

The pathway created an advantage for her because it was a ten minutes' walk to attend lectures.

Occupants were living in the rooms based on the decision and the needs of the landlords.

The landlords of the boy's quarters were lecturers occupying the central accommodation.

The BQ occupants were a mixture of post-graduate and undergraduate students. There were seven rooms on each side.

The rooms correspond to the number of flats and houses around the street.
There was a tree next to her room, which was closer to the shared bathroom.

Chloe enjoyed the evenings cooking and chatting with her neighbours. But she had to accommodate their different lifestyles.

She aimed at presenting the Saviour by her routine.

They nicknamed her 'Holy Dimples.'

Independence came with a price. She could not run to Mama Joe as often.

Chloe now has to deal with situations on her own, such as the news about Akin (her Library friend).

Mama Joe saw him on her way home and informed her.

*"Akin has been in town for a while? He didn't bother to contact me? It's strange. School is still in session."*

Chloe considered as she stared on her phone. Her heartbeat in fast pulse recalled all her memories with Akin.

She had called him several times with no response.

Many waters had passed under the bridge; Chloe was not sure where to pick up things with him.

It's been six years, but her heart still longed after him.

Chloe could not deny the excitement she felt.

She called Akin's brother to confirm at once. It could be one of the few visits he had had since he gained admission.

This time, it was not good news.

Akin decided not to consider the Saviour for himself, as Chloe had advised but joined a cult on campus.

A cult was something she could never imagine he would do. Considering he was quiet, intelligent and came from a well-mannered family.

Unfortunately, for him, the university excommunicated him and was back home for good. Chloe was sad and longed to visit with him.

*"Maybe a hug would make things better, or better still a slap for being so foolish as to get carried away with bad friends".*

Thinking about him upset her!

The next evening, there was a knock on her room. She opened the door; Akin visited Chloe with a lady.

"Hello, Stranger!" She said, opening the door for her visitors.

Akin rushed toward her with a hug.

"Hi, friend. I am sorry I have not been in touch."

"Is that why you came with someone, so I don't roast you alive," Chloe said, laughing.

"Touché! You are right again", Akin giggled, acknowledging the gentle tease from Chloe.

"She is here to calm you down and stop you from getting too mad with me," he teased back.

"Though I need help. I need a place for my lady friend to pass the night; home is difficult now."

Chloe was happy and sad for him at the same time. Although she didn't ask, she assumed he had found a lady to make him happy, and this made her glad.

She avoided questions about the lady, although she felt a cold breeze of Akin's departure on her heart.

Chloe swung into action and made a place for the lady to spend the night with her.

Alas, she had to close the door forever in her heart to forget him. He would always be a friend but not a special friend.

Chloe spoke to her neighbour, who provided a place for Akin to spend the night.

Late into the night, Chloe and Akin sat on the porch under the bright moonlight.

He apologised for disappointing. The trust of his family and Chloe, when Akin went off to the university.

He relayed to her the fun he believed he would have when introduced to the gang.

Akin would be friends with the rich, firm and powerful guys on campus; the crowd would fear him.

He lost his bearing and the sanity he brought from home. Soon, he went partying, taking drugs, having sex, drinking with the boys and fighting with rival gangs.

One of their altercations with a rival gang got out of control. Akin's cult group killed a student who was a son of one of the prominent politicians.

Although they tried to keep things quiet and denied that the attack had ever happened, the truth spilt out.

Akin's saving grace was that he was ill on the night of the attack and could not go out with the gang.

Still, that did not exonerate him from guilt entirely as he was part of the cult.

A few weeks into the investigation, the police knocked at their doors.

They arrested all the boys in the rooms, including Akin. Admitting, he was not involved as the crow flies in the crime that night.

He had to come clean to his family, and he went to prison for a short while.

The university suspended him for being part of a gang — a crime against the university rules.

After the investigations, Akin was later released from detention, but Akin was back to square one. What a shame!

"Why didn't you listen to me! I kept trying to help you, but you kept pulling away," Chloe exclaimed in a frustrated tone.

Akin held her hands stuttering.

"Please don't make it worse than it is already. I have to pay a high price for refusing to accept the price the Saviour had already paid. I pray He forgives me."

Chloe held out her hands to calm his stuttering.

"He will. He loves you still. It doesn't have anything to do with who you are or what you've done. But because of what He did for you,"

Chloe added with a hug.

He rested his head on her shoulder.

Akin sobbed in silence like a baby. She felt deep empathy for him.

*"Maybe I could have supported him more. I tried my best."*

After a while of sharing a sober moment, Chloe asked,

"How is your family coping? What would you do next? Please open up to me."

She urged him to be honest with her.

"I broke my family. Not sure where to begin." Akin muttered as he cleared his throat.

"Start somewhere; we have all night." She looked straight into his eyes, searching for the truth.

"My family has fallen apart, seemed mum and dad would separate soon. They blame each other for not providing the right directions I needed in life."

"Is that true?"

"Of course not! They tried. Unprejudiced, like my situation with you, I refused to listen. They took me to church, Sunday school when I was young. I rejected it, I rebelled."

"I understand now," she sighed.

"No, you can't! I wasted my life. Not only will I have to start again. I have lost trust before the family. "

"The black sheep, right?" she hinted, rubbing her hands on his lap.

"That's an understatement; my mum is still ready to stand by me. You know mothers would always do that. Dad is unapproachable at the moment. All my siblings are trying to forgive me little by little."

"How do you mean?" She enquired.

"To begin with, none visited me in the police detention."

"O dear, I can only imagine."

"Since my family had noticed, I have become sober, on my return home. We are working on our relationships."

"I am rather sorry. Do you know I visited several times? I worried about you. You never replied to my letters. Mama Joe prayed so much for you. "

"Her prayers must have worked, I have a second chance to begin again," Akin laughed.

He reached out his hands holding hers; he continued, "Thank you, you are a true friend."

"Remember, friends, are not only those that are there with you in good times. But those that hold you through the bad times and the good times," Chloe reassured him.

"I tried to be there for all my friends. But I can only do much, especially when I have often being pushed away all the time."

"This time, I have learnt my lessons. Those that want the best for me are the hardest nut to crack like you."

"How?"

Chloe interrupted him.

"The letter you wrote to me. I thought you didn't want me around you. Now I understand you wanted to be a friend in season and out of season."

"How?"

Chloe enquired further with a perplexed face.

"I wanted a friend for a season. I am glad you didn't give in to my demands. Who knows, you might have compromised your promises to the Saviour."

"True, back then, it was hard for me to decide between what I wanted and what I needed."

She shook her head in agreement.

"In conclusion, all things work together for good, that includes the good, the bad and the ugly things."

Chloe held on to her friend in a close embrace.

It was a hard lesson for Akin. Chloe told him about the changes in her situation.

Such as, her decision to live independently of the rest of her family, so they could all have their privacy.

Akin became concerned about the cost of living alone.

She reminded him she had been fending for herself since she left secondary school, almost seven years ago.

"It would not be different," said Chloe.

She would only need to trust her Saviour more.

Chloe told Akin about an encounter she had had with a total stranger.

The man she met on the street while in the company of some friends. He held her hand and told her Chloe would gain admission into the university. The period she had not even passed her university entry.

Chloe said the man stated that her Eternal Lover said,

**"He will take care of you. He has taken care of you. Until you complete your degree, the rest of your life, He will justify as he promised. "**

Chloe's words made meaning to Akin at last. Before now, he had brushed aside the ideas of her 'Saviour' until he got himself into trouble with the law.

It was a defining moment for them as friends.

To Akin, he was to seek the Saviour, and for Chloe, it brought a fresh determination to love Him more with all her heart.

Nothing would change her steadfast love for her Saviour.

If only she could sort out one thing - the pain of the past and its effect on future relationships.

Chloe believed Akin would make better choices for his future. She prayed for him and headed for bed.

Early the next morning after breakfast. Before Akin and his friend said their "goodbyes", Chloe had an unexpected visit from Mife (her secret admirer).

Mife showed up unannounced parading himself in front of Akin with a sense of ownership over her.

Chloe, even though, was enjoying her relationship with him.

As with Akin, it seemed a pace with him would be a poor decision.

Tobi (Chloe's friend) had commented on Mife's attraction to Chloe. Tobi kept urging her to reveal her feelings for Mife.

He was shy and quiet, yet she found him controlling, and friendship with him became more demanding each day.

She was not willing to hurt him; considering her experience with Frank.

She tried to give Mife the attention he required most times.

But,

"This morning's visit was unwelcomed," Chloe upsetting brainwaves raged.

Chloe knew that sharing her opinions about Mife means risking her integrity.

She deflected Tobi's enquiry by encouraging her to go out with Mife herself. Mife was great at using Tobi to get at her.

It was becoming difficult to see their friendship as mere friendship. Because of the several gifts, Mife showered on Chloe.

There was nothing more to the relationship. But to Mife, she seemed to be the woman made for him. Would this work?

# UNEXPECTED HAPPENS

*The lot is cast into the lap,*
*but every decision is from the Lord.*

One-night Chloe was preparing for her usually two hours' study when she heard a knock on her door at about ten pm.

"I am not expecting a visitor this late," she pondered.

Opening the door, a gentleman from her church met her.

After exchanging greetings with Chloe, the gentleman said,

"The pastor wants you in the church."

Chloe enquired further, concerned she might be in trouble. She must have to defend herself in front of the church leadership.

"Could it be about her circle of friends?" she asked herself.

The gentleman walked toward his car while Chloe

locked her doors.

They drove for about 20 mins in grave silence. Chloe started praying in her mind that it would be good news. She wouldn't be able to bear any bad news.

"What have I done again?"

Her mind pondered as they drove into the church. From the dashboard reflections, she saw a glimpse.

She could see the pastor and his wife sitting on the pavement, in front of the church looking gloomy.

She came out and ran and knelt to greet them. They welcomed her with fervour and asked her to sit between them.

Both were holding her hands with concern; the pastor broke the stillness and spoke at last.

"Chloe, are you aware that your mum had been on her usual mission trip volunteering over the last week?"

His wife added,

"We were glad she was doing what she knows how to do well – cooking and serving."

Chloe replied,

"Yes, sir, I also know that she travelled with Sarah to visit a family member. I could not bid them farewell. I had a test this morning.

Chloe continued with trembling;

"Several times, I tried her phone; she switched it off. The last time we spoke was yesterday; she sounded excited about the visit. I communicated with Joe after class. He informed me they had travelled. She left me with kisses from Joe."

Chloe started feeling uncomfortable with her sweaty hands.

"Indeed!" he continued.

"On their way, there was an accident."…

There was a long pause.

His wife added, "Your beloved mother passed away. Sarah is alive, but in a critical condition in the hospital."

Like a statue, Chloe froze, speechless, motionless. Mama Joe's words rang in her head like a resounding bell.

*"If I would sin against the lover of my soul, I would rather that He takes me today so that I would be in His presence forever. His presence is more important to me than silver or gold."*

Mama Joe said this each time her children comforted her. They had promised to take care of and protect her when they became rich.

Without emotion, Chloe whispered.

"Mama Joe said it. She said it! She said she wanted the Saviour to take her if He knows she would sin against Him, and He did. He forgot to take me along."

Tears finally rolled down Chloe's cheeks.

The pastor sighed and held Chloe close to his heart. He reminded her,

"The Saviour gives and takes away; blessed be His name."

"Yes, I know," Chloe continued.

"She would not see my children. I wouldn't take care of her. Mama Joe has suffered too much. He should not have taken her away so soon."

The pastors further reminded her.

"A few years earlier, Mama Joe had a stroke. Despite been hospitalised with a blood pressure of 245/95mmHg. He completely restored her to us. She lived like an angel among us the remaining time she had, and He took her back."

"It is true," Chloe murmured between her tears.

After a while, the pastor said,

"I do not think it's alright for you to be by yourself tonight. Your brother, Joe, had to travel to identify her body. We made arrangements for you to stay with us. We have communicated with him, and he should be in town tomorrow. We advised him we would break the news to you."

Chloe, as usual, tried not to show any sign of weakness.

She replied,

"Pastor, I am okay. I will go home. I want to be by myself and worship the Saviour for giving me a wonderful angel as a mother."

Getting home, Chloe took time to worship as she had promised; she knew it would never be the same without her mother.

*"Who would be my confidant? Who would laugh with me as she does? Who will understand me? Who would fight for me on her knees? Who would love me as she does? Who would read the Bible with me? Imagine, she never stepped into a school. Yet she taught herself to read the Bible without a doubt, with her children's support. Who would ever be like my mother?"*

Questions after questions poured into her heart with not one answer. Mama Joe did not even get to see her graduate, with the first-class she had promised.

As tears kept flowing, on her knees, Chloe vowed to be the best Mama Joe meant her to be. Because of the angel that walked through life with her called Mama Joe!

Chloe's first attempt to get out of bed was about noon the next day. Her body ached with pain.

*"It's a dream! Right? The Saviour would bring back Mama Joe. Yes, he will, she can't leave like this."*

She wept as she dragged herself to the toilet. She was glad there was no one around.

It's close to the semester exams, and everyone must have gone to read. Chloe crawled into bed, folded herself up like a hermit crab. She sobbed for one more goodnight from her mother.

Images of Mama Joe dotted around her. At sunset, her stomach ached with pain. Her throat had dried up like a parched desert screaming for a quench for her dryness. She prayed no one would come near her door.

At that moment, she heard the door.

Covering her head with a pillow, she shouted,

"Go away! I am not in a great place to receive friends."

Remi called out to her

"Chloe listen, Joe called Chuks and I. He told us about mummy. We have been trying to reach you. We know now why you were not at the department all day."

Chuks added, "Can we come in?"

"Go away!" she revolted.

"Let me mourn alone," she sobbed at full volume.

Remi and Chuks ignored her resistance yells and opened the door.

The door was dim with pain, smells with a mix of her sweat and uncirculated air.

Remi rushed to her and cuddled her into his hands, crying with her.

Chuks open the curtain and windows to provide fresh air and light into the room.

Chuks joined in and echoed,

"It *would* be alright; Mama Joe was our mum too, we feel the pain."

"Have you eaten anything today?" he offered her water.

His question went unanswered. Chuks got Chloe

something to bite from the refrigerator.

The news spread like wildfire; she was fragile and vulnerable and had lost a significant player in her life.

Chloe phone rang for the forty-second time. Chuks picked the caller while Remi held her close to his bosom.

That evening, Seyi and his pal, Tommy walked into the church at the announcement of the passing away of Mama Joe. They headed back to Chloe's because of the heart-breaking news.

Seyi shared his intimate encounters with Mama Joe. While Tommy sat in silence, watching Chloe with intensity.

In the next two hours, Chloe filled her room with sympathisers.

She had a vague recollection about acknowledgement who visited.

Her mind wondered about the precious memories she shared with an extraordinary mother.

Her friends took turns to be with her day and night.

She knew they loved her, but no amount of attention she receives can take the dark shades of her loss away.

She faced her deep bowel of grief each day.

A few days later, Joe identified his mother's body. Chloe and her brothers had to bury their mother with the support of the church family.

Her two brothers devastated and confused mourned mama ceaseless with few words.

Chloe prayed like a ghost when she heard her father harsh words blaming her uncle for his wife's death.

*"I pray, Uncle Steve would not blame himself for the death of Mama for the rest of his life. According to Papa Joe's condemnation."*

Sarah remained in the hospital in a critical condition for the foreseeable future.

The complications from the accident had left her with fractured bones. She would need several surgical procedures.

According to the consultant, after the operation, Sarah would have to overgo years of physiotherapy. Acknowledging she prayed the Saviour for a quick recovery.

Chloe heartbroken about Sarah reflected.

*"Poor girl! Despite all she has been through, she's still encouraging us."*

Sarah asked the rest of her siblings to think about the hope of seeing her someday with the Saviour.

Days turned into weeks and weeks into months. Each of the siblings mourned Mama Joe's death in isolation.

Deep down in Chloe's mind, she wished 'her' Mama Joe could walk through the door.

Her circle of friends kept her company and brought much-needed comfort.

Soon, her smiles came back, and she got back the rhythm of her life. Chloe's church and fellowship made sure someone was not far away.

Reminding her that "His promises are yes and amen."

Supo, Remi, Chuks, Tobi, Seyi and Sheryl (her older friend), formed a ring of care around Chloe.

It was during this period that she grew closer to one of her friends, Tommy from the drama group.

Tommy was now a postgraduate student in physics.

Compared to Seyi, he was quiet and only spoke when he needed to.

He smiled along whenever there was a heated debate or discussion in Chloe's room.

On personal interaction with Chloe, they acted like "Tom and Jerry."

Chloe had provided a rationale to herself that Supo, Remi, Seyi and Chuks are in fact brothers to her.

Still, she could not define if there was anything more to her relationship with Tommy.

She proposed not to push any boundaries beyond friendship.

Except, if any of them redefines the terms of their friendship.

Tommy was different. In the absence of Mama Joe, she longed for a companion.

Tommy was always in the company of Seyi when he visited.

Chloe finally asked him why he wouldn't visit her alone.

Tommy responded with "Nothing" with his eyes blinking as usual when he becomes uncomfortable.

"Your 'nothing' seems pregnant," Chloe teased him. But he would not give in to the sentiments of her line of questioning.

It was strange to Chloe because they appeared to be a close company in church.

Chloe wondered in despair about is continuous reservation.

He is shy without the company of other friends around her.

Nothing makes a handsome, intelligent, God-fearing guy like Tommy say, "Nothing!"

With tears dripping from her eyes, she taught about the need for someone more than a friend.

Images of Tommy wandered around her mind as a torment.

*"Is it that Tommy liked Chloe and was too shy to visit alone, or he was only... I can't even deal with this right now..."*

Chloe exclaimed, adjusting herself on the reading seat.

*"I am meant to be studying,"* her mind quizzed her.

*"Okay, he is compassionate because Mama Joe left me,"* Chloe sobbed regurgitating the pain of her loss.

Chloe was sure she liked his personality, and they seemed to complement each other.

*"I would not mind going out with him,"* she continued her line of thought.

Was he ready or willing to go out with her? Will she be able to find out?

# SEEKING COMFORT

*My comfort in my suffering is this:*
*Your promise preserves my life.*

By a hair's breadth, a year after her mother died, Chloe felt a lump in her right breast while having her bath.

She screamed,

*"This can't be happening to me! Aunty Sade! Was this what she felt before the doctor diagnosed her?"*

Aunty Sade was a beloved sister who passed away about ten years earlier, after a fight with breast cancer.

*"Would I also die in ostentatious circumstances?"* Part of her was happy.

She would see Mama Joe in heaven. But another part said,

*"I have not lived my life; that is selfish. Consider all*

*those that love you."*

Chloe had a chat with her brother Joe and booked an appointment at the university clinic.

Immediately, she referred herself to the oncology department at the teaching hospital.

The doctor carried out some physical tests and proceeded to a breast scan.

As the trials progressed, Chloe became apprehensive about the outcome.

Two weeks later, the diagnosis was Fibrocystic breast disease.

The condition is usually benign. The lump was massive; consequently, the doctor recommended surgery immediately.

The doctor advised she discussed with her family first before taking any decision.

Apart from her siblings, Chloe remembered Supo, who had gone through trauma and ended up with a scar.

It would only be fair to let him know and get some reassurance that all would be well.

She met with Supo and opened up about her situation. He did not seem surprised.

He knew it would have taken all that she had to open up her vulnerability to him.

As a result, he would take everything about this announcement invariable. He put his hands around Chloe's neck, speaking helpful as usual.

"This too would pass. Soon you wouldn't even remember it happened."

She cried

"The scar would say so," shaking her head.

Holding her even closer to himself, Supo whispered:

"You are more beautiful with the scar."

She clung to him, saying,

"Thank you for reminding me of my words."

One other confidant that Chloe had been a professor in her department.

Mrs Longe had taken on the role of a mother since Mama Joe passed away.

She encouraged and supported her to be the best they thought her to be.

She also spoke to her husband, and they prayed with her that all would go well with the surgery.

✿ ✿ ✿

Chloe had the operation a week later, which turned out to be in part successful.

The doctors could not remove all the lumps without causing a long-term effect.

Her oncologist informed her of the chunks embedded within the breast tissues. He recommended regular check-ups.

That evening, Chloe got a call from a landlord that Joe was in his house with Papa Joe. "Papa Joe!" she exclaimed.

*"What does he want from me?... How did he know I had surgery earlier today?... We have not spoken in seven years?... Did Joe inform him?... I instructed all my siblings not to communicate my personal affairs with him."*

She, with difficulty, got out of bed with her sore chest. Walking out of her compound, Joe hurried toward her.

"How are you, dear?" Joe called out to her.

"I have been praying all day, hope it went well."

"Joe, I'm okay. I will live."

"Definitely! You will," Joe replied.

"What is he doing here, who told him I was in the hospital, did you?"

Chloe voiced her concerns to Joe while staring at her

father from a distance.

"Chloe, listen, relax! I never told him. I am as surprised as yourself when he showed up at my door."

"What!" Chloe exclaimed.

They walked toward Papa Joe, who was leaning on Joe's car.

Joe continued, "He heard you were in a hospital for surgery this morning, and he wanted to make sure you were alright."

"Alright! What does he mean? He wanted me to die like Mama, right, did He? What does he want after seven years of abandonment?" Chloe protested.

"Don't worry, baby sister. I am here with you; let's find out what he came for."

Chloe tied her tongue in the presence of Pape Joe. Papa Joe questioned her about the circumstances that led to the surgery.

Joe replied to all the questions on her behalf.
His visit was brief; they shared nothing in common. Like strangers, Papa Joe gave Chloe a cold hug as his goodbye.

Chloe watched him in the distance as Joe whispered into her ears.

"I would be back, let me drop him at home."
Chloe's feet stoke to the ground in shock,

"How did this man get to know about my breast incident? Now I know, he is a weirdo."

A tap on her shoulder from her landlord brought her back to her reality.

"I reason you need to get some rest. Chloe, we are supporting you all the way."

He walked her to the room to rest.

✿ ✿ ✿

Recovering from the new, unexpected life event. Chloe pondered once more:

*"Deformed teeth, fear of loving, now breast again? Should I shut the door to the ideas of a fruitful relationship forever?"*

Despite this, Tommy's image kept flashing through her mind.

*"Don't get any crazy ideas,"* she told herself after she learned Tommy was going out of the country for his PhD.

If only she had someone she could confide in about the secret fears or about the feelings she had towards Tommy.

*"Tommy was a comfort in the absence of Mama Joe."*

Chloe mulled over, shutting down her reflections of him.

Her mind flashed back to one conversation she had with him. His enlarged pupils stared into her eyes after dinner.

It raged with a sense of entitlement for answers.

"Chloe, we all had the best of Mama Joe while she was with us."

His eyes still fixed on her, he continued,

"Don't you think she would have loved us to live our lives with fulfilment at every moment, as she did?"

Chloe pulled herself somewhat away from his gaze, used her arm to drop her pen from the table.

Reaching out to pick it, Tommy met her halfway. He touched the palm of her hands, arousing her five senses.

"I'm sorry, didn't mean to do that," he said, minimising eye contact with her.

Nevertheless, Chloe saw the side smile of his face.

"I know you didn't mean sorry. We should agree on one point; you enjoyed the feel of your touch on mine."

She responded with a determination to the profound denial of his affection toward her.

"Tommy, I know Mama Joe would have wanted us to live our lives."

Standing up to clear the table, she continued.

"I have faith that she would have also loved me to keep my friendships as open as possible."

"Yes, she would definitely like that."

"So, Tom, could you be free with me, I don't bite. True, I may well have feeling running all over my veins. But be sure, I have boundaries to keep to myself and the saviour. I don't intend to break the promises I made to myself."

Tommy adjusted himself reassured in the presence of a good friend. He cleared his throat and said,

"Thank you. I agree that I needed more assurance than you. I appreciate you from the bottom of my heart. You are a rare woman!"

With unease brewing within her, she picked a non-existing fluff off her clothing.

Chloe smiled and said,

"We all need that, especially when we don't know whom we are dealing with."

In her mind, she questioned,

*"Who am I dealing with here?* Mama Joe, you have the right answer about every one of my friends. I want you back."

Her eyes swollen with tears.

"Chloe, did I say anything wrong?" He stood up and handed over his handkerchief to her.

"No, you did nothing wrong, I miss mum." She interrupted him, taking the handkerchief to clean her tears.

"You know, I would always be a shoulder for you to cry on, I am here when you need me. Chloe, you have good friends surrounding you."

Moving her head at a snail's pace on his shoulder, Chloe sobbed non-stop for her Mama Joe.

200

Tommy seemed to have become more relaxed around Chloe over the following months.

He visited on his own, especially when taking breaks from studying.

They grew fond of each other's company, even though they knew Tommy would leave to study in another country.

It was not surprising that Tommy discussed his intimate desires - his family and career.

She got more endeared to him. She knew her feelings for him were growing.

It worried her that his family religious denomination would be a barrier.

Tommy's religious denomination identification was known for their conservatism.

Their women could not wear make-up, jewellery or other showy apparels. She was not sure where he stood or his convictions vis-à-vis these issues.

Knowing his family belonged to the same denomination, it was easy to assume the worst about him. She convinced herself to explore and believe.

The Saviour would bring the convictions needed to move to the next level.

Several times, Chloe would start a dispute, to understand Tommy stands about his conservative background.

He would always deflect from his opinion, acknowledging his family's position. It was challenging to realise his views about her.

In the blink of an eye, Tommy left the country with no notice.

He showed no interest in building a lifelong relationship with her.

At least, a goodbye should have been appropriate, why would he leave without a note?

In any case, she was glad she had his email, an open-door to keep contact.

Chloe laid on her bed, thinking about the times they spent together.

"He was a great comfort. I have lost another unique part of me. Will there be a future Tommy and Chloe?

She sighed, reflecting on all the losses and gains of her life.

After daydreaming of being Mrs Tommy, Chloe slept off.

The next day started with him on her mind. She kept believing in keeping open communications with him.

One day, it would create a situation to have a conversation about the future.

She feared the feelings she was developing for Tommy might not be reciprocal.

# TOO LONG TOO FAR

*All the ways of the Lord are loving and
faithful toward those who keep
the demands of his covenant.*

Shortly after Tommy travelled, Mife visited Chloe. He informed her he *would* be going for the next six months for his post-graduate fieldwork. He looked lost; it was so difficult to figure him out.

Sometimes, the soft part of him prevails. Other times, he is controlling. She was glad; he was leaving.

She needed a fresh breath, clean air. She couldn't figure out why she felt choked around Mife.

Soon after he left, "Mr Perfect" came along. Max was a

postgraduate student who worked in the same office as Sheryl, one of Chloe's older friends.

Sheryl had been excellent support for Chloe when her mother passed away.

Mama Joe had deepened their friendship.

Chloe usually popped into her office to say "Hi" from time to time.

They would encourage each other about life and relationships.

On a visit to Sheryl's office one day, Max walked up to Chloe and blocked her path. In benevolent, she asked him to step aside, but he refused.

He was adamant that she would have to chat with him before she could leave.

All the while he spoke, Chloe did not look at him as the crow flies.

She later asked,

"Okay, why do you want me to chat with you?"

He reached out his hands and touched her hands. That was when she looked at him.

Max had an exciting look. As a man from her dreams, he was tall about 6.5 feet (1.98 m) and much taller than all the men she had ever known. He had tanned skin with distinctive eyeglasses.

He stepped aside and said,

"I see you each time you come in to see Sheryl; you look like an interesting, smart lady. You are exquisite; Can I know you better?"

Chloe smiled.

"Look at that! See the dimples," he exclaimed.

Chloe, blushing, held out her hands to reply,

"Thank you. I'm Chloe and as for the dimples, get used to them. They aren't going anywhere."

"I'm Max," he replied immediately.

"I suppose you were shy."

"I am until you get to know my name; afterwards, I am not," replied Chloe.

"Alright," Max said.

She guessed he was not expecting that. They shook hands, and she headed off to see Sheryl but unfortunately; she was not available.

"This is to Max's advantage, I guess," contemplated Chloe.

Meeting new people was her speciality. They exchanged information about each other for the next two hours.

Thank goodness! Chloe had finished her exams. Thus, she had all the time in the world to meet someone new.

The greetings turned into a walk to her room and lunch.

He finally left her room late in the evening.

Each day Max would meet up with Chloe and walk her to her department, and soon he became a regular companion for her.

Chloe was enjoying the company of her new friend. Although, deep within, she longed for the company of Tommy and Remi, who seemed like her next-to-mother comfort.

✿ ✿ ✿

Chloe had to learn to manage the loss of her dear friend, Remi.

"Remi right! Rem, my beloved friend" She mourned.

He distanced himself from her because of a tiny disagreement they had.

It was the least expected. Chloe tried to express her displeasure at being stood up for an appointment they had planned.

Remi provided excuses rather than an apology.

In response, Chloe said, "If I were your wife, will you

keep giving excuses rather than say sorry?"

To Chloe's surprise, Remi replied with all of a sudden, "Goodnight," as a timely response and refused to visit or speak to her.

She had tried several times to reach out and talk to him, but it upset him to handle the discussion. She missed her dear friend.

Heartbroken, she deliberated.

*"Could a statement about the way he treated a friend break up their friendship?"*

Chloe remembered she said,

"Is that the way you would treat me if I were your wife?" Should her statement cost her a dear friend?

She accepted it as a consequence of being friends with someone younger.

He would not admit any form of feeling for her or accept he had fallen in love with her.

Remi could have assured himself; there was no possibility they could be together forever.

Within four weeks, Max discussions became rather more personal and affectionate towards Chloe.

He prompted several talks about his dream wife, what his home would be like with kids running around.

They discussed how he would handle conflict if she married him.

He loved politics, and as she was knowledgeable; so, they enjoyed the arguments that came along with it.

Although Max stated he was a child of the Saviour, she was sceptical.

Chloe had met no one close to him other than his colleagues, that could confirm what she knew about him.

His affectionate gifts and words in stages started the

quest to find the real Max.

It was too quick to be authentic.

Mife, on his return from the fieldwork, got wind of the new guy on the block.

Mife started pursuing Chloe in a hostile way.

He tried to get more of her attention and a few times, Mife met Max in Chloe's room.

She enjoyed the rivalry between them. She felt like a 'sought-after', 'special' and 'irresistible', 'selfish' lady.

Chloe broke the ice and offered some entertainment while maintaining a friendly atmosphere.

On one occasion, Mife's decision to leave first helped to defuse the tension.

It was such a relief! Chloe walked him out of her room and on return found Max on bended knee with a proposal ring.

"Will you marry me, my dimples?"

"Chloe has finally arrived!" she screamed inside her reasoning.

Hang on a minute!

There was a check, "Who is Max?"

She had not found the right answer, and the relationship had only begun.

Chloe thanked him for the proposal.

She explained that she needed to talk to her Saviour about him before deciding.

One evening after Max had left for the day, Mife showed up at her room and opened up about his intentions.

He reminded her, "Chloe, I have known you and

watched you enjoy personal time in the university.

I have not burdened you with the need to have you to myself."

Chloe interrupted him.

"Mife, you know I would not allow you. I love myself too much to become a burden by you."

Mife remained calm and quiet while she continued,

"I'm sorry! I didn't mean to make you less important. You are important to me; you are a dear friend."

He smiled and said,

"Chloe, I want to marry you."

"Whoop! I didn't see that coming," Chloe exclaimed with her heart racing.

"Mife," she carried on,

"You know it can't work, we have talked about it over and over again. The foundation of our faith is different. I like you as a friend. If I have given you a sign, there was anything more to it. I am sorry."

Chloe kept on, "You told me in absolute terms, you can't choose my Saviour; my Saviour is jealous. He would only permit me to marry someone that would love and serve Him like me."

By this time, tears had swelled in Mife's eyes. Chloe fell on her knees before him, hugging him.

"Mife, I like you, but we can't be together."

Mife got himself together and insisted,

"I would not change my religious denomination. Any lady that would marry me would have to accept and join my denomination."

Chloe, who was not surprised, by his display of pride, replied,

"You know I used to be in same religious denomination before. I am not anymore and don't intend to go back."

After Mife left, Chloe knew she had to shut the door of her heart to him. He tried to get in, but it would never be possible.

She tried protecting him from further hurt by not keeping in contact with him.

He was such a cool, calm, emotional and fragile guy. She refused to see him or respond to his calls and texts.

One evening, she came home to see a note, it read:

"Chloe, I am sick. Dying to see you or I would die, Love M".

Chloe felt responsible for putting him in this state. The impression he got that they could become more than friends was false.

At other times, she justified herself by stating, "I have been closer to other guys. Why did they not take it the wrong way?"

A few days later, Tobi showed up at her door with another note from Mife.

"Please see me, (with a love-shaped M,)" it read.

Tobi smiled and said, "You guys sort yourselves out!"

Chloe reassured Tobi, "I have informed him it wouldn't work, but he thinks otherwise."

Swinging her around Tobi, she continued,

"He would rather stick to his stubborn stance. Mife expects any woman whom he wants to marry to take his faith."

"It seems selfish," Tobi continued.

"If he does this now, what would he expect or demand from me when I marry him,"

Tobi laughed comically.

Chloe suggested Mife to Tobi as a perfect partner.

"You guys were already close friends." Chloe teased.

Tobi laughed it off.

"No, thanks but thanks," she replied.

That evening after Tobi left Chloe's room, she thought of finally visiting Mife to bury the hatchet.

She took a cab to Mife's postgraduate residential hall.

At the entrance, she met Yinka.

"I know you," they both said at the same time.

Yinka was her mentor's son (Mrs Longe).

"What are you doing here?" Chloe asked.

"I live here," he replied.

"What are you doing here? I know you are not a postgraduate student. Are you already coming to see them? Hmm! Hmm,"

Yinka laughed, clearing his throat.

"You are not serious! Yes, I came to see a friend. Simply a friend, nothing attached,"

Chloe replied, defending her actions.

"Wait, don't tell me I am not old enough to do that. O, dear! Please don't tell my mummy," she pleaded light-heartedly.

Yinka kept giggling and said, "This is a friend, Folu."

Folu stretched out his hands to shake hers and said,

"These dimples are killing me."

Chloe laughed.

"Don't die yet. When I leave, you can take your life. In a minute, wait!"

They all laughed, exchanged numbers, and parted ways.

That evening was one of the most boring evenings in Chloe's exciting life.

Her meditations kept moving from Tommy to Max to Yinka.

"But why, Yinka? I must admit he has a lovely smile.

I am curious why he was pretending he doesn't know me. I have been meeting him in his mother's office all this while," she deliberated.

Mife had nothing to offer her. He was too quiet and sulking like a little child.

She wanted to hold his hands and comfort him. Yet, she was not willing to open a door that would be difficult for her to shut.

After two hours, she left him, hoping it was with a firm understanding that things would not be the same again.

They were honest friends, nothing more.

She had the usual visit from Supo the next day, who knew all her friends.

She told him all about the various drama with her relationships.

With a straight face, Supo smiled and said: "Beauty, I am glad you are alright.

The Saviour will, with awareness, guard your heart."

Words Supo said with intense passion in his eyes for the first time.

Supo left a strange impression on her. Where, does he belong in the scope of her heart?

He never seems to bother her mind like the others. But she knew amongst all her friends he was the most reliable.

# HARD PLACE

*The Lord is close to the broken-hearted and*
*saves those who are crushed in spirit.*

Chloe knew her fun period was getting closer to an end;
she was in her pre-final year.

Since she started university, her landscape of friends had
changed. Her mind was in a turmoil, with Tommy away.

Max's proposal brought an extreme confusion of whom
he was in actuality.

And Yinka flashing on her mind sometimes.

She had struggled with making choices; only the Saviour
could direct her.

She did what she knew best; to the Saviour.

As usual, Chloe would sense that the Saviour was talking to her through the pages of His words.

She was flipping through while thinking about her reply to Max.

Although not confused about her feelings for Tommy. She bothered about how she would fit into his religious denomination.

That's if she could ever contemplate being that kind of person.

"Would it be that hard?" Chloe teased herself.

Chloe came across a passage, where the Saviour described His intentional choice.

Jacob over Esau, despite Esau, being the older one. In her experience, Max was quite older than Tommy.

His sovereignty over the choice popped out as the passage emphasised.

A man's opinion could not influence His.

Chloe understood the meaning and implication of the first part of the journey - His sovereignty.

Chloe seldom did not put much consideration into it. She trusted God to make known the right choice between the 'Jacob' and the 'Esau' among the beloved men around her.

Max did not show up as expected, and Chloe had not seen him for some days.

Even though her heart longed for his company, she knew the dangers of putting too many expectations on men.

As a woman, the culture expects you to be the 'catch' and not the one doing the 'catching'.

After two weeks, she popped in to see Max.

She met his colleagues on her way out, who informed her that Max would not be returning.

He had finished his programme and had moved back home, in the eastern part of the country.

It shocked Chloe! She asked what he meant by 'back home'?

He informed her that his wedding was in a fortnight.

To clarify his statement, he took her hands. Led Chloe to the notice board, which posted his wedding invitation.

Although it was a rude shock, it didn't traumatise her world.

The words of the Saviour came rushing to her mind; *"Jacob I chose, Esau I hate."*

She comforted herself immediately; Max was the Esau.

Moments later, she proceeded to Sheryl's office and informed her about her ordeal with Max.

Surprised by the news, Sheryl tried to understand the reasons for his actions.

"Guess he wanted a cheap fling but met the wrong lady. Be encouraged."

She continued,

"And beware of wolves in sheep's clothing."

Chloe kept those words close to her heart as she thanked the Saviour for her deliverance.

The puzzle seemed not completed.

There appeared to be a fulfilment of one part of His words.

The other part had eluded Chloe.

She wanted to know if Tommy represented Jacob. Tommy is too far to reach.

She wouldn't be able to understand what's happening in his beautiful mind.

Will Chloe learn to trust one more time?

Chloe didn't consider talking to the Saviour.

She weighed up a way to make things easier for herself.

Chloe spoke to Seyi, Tommy's friend instead. She discussed her feelings and persuasions towards Tommy.

"Maybe Tommy had confided in him, and Seyi might give a piece of advice or two."

Seyi did not act 'too surprised' as Chloe had expected. To be candid, he had wondered who would tell him first, knowing the ways of his two friends.

"That is comforting." Chloe reflected.

But "What if Tommy's thinking differs from tip to toe from Seyi?" she argued as the war brewed within her. She concluded on a truce idea.

"That was I intend Seyi needed to find out." Chloe would hate to get hurt in the process.

Chloe kept constant communication with Tommy, who was about 6,600miles (ca. 10,622 km) away.

Sometimes it was difficult; it cost so much to go to the Internet café to send emails or chat with him.

Chloe soon discovered it was cheaper to visit the internet cafe at night, due to the flat rate.

She invested in keeping in touch with him.

Most times, Tommy responded well. But sometimes his response was as though Chloe was a bother to him.
She overlooked these awkward responses.

Chloe, on purpose, tried not to read meaning into them. She denied they could be the wrong signs.

Often, she would relay her misgivings about Tommy's responses to Seyi.

His answers often reassured her. He reminded her to trust the Saviour:
"If he said it, He would do it."

Sometimes she wrote her feelings in her journal. Longing to be with Tommy, she reminded herself of the fun times they had together.

Chloe remembered the walks they had in the evenings. How he questioned her with a stern, gazing into her eyes in despair.

"What kind of man would you like to marry?"

"You!" Chloe wanted to scream out.

Nonetheless, she, in a friendly way, looked away though she was shy narrating the features she wanted in her man.

*"I have told no one these, not even Mama Joe,"* she reflected as she spoke to him.

*"How does he get me to be so open and dropping my guard around him?"*

My man! Must be fun to be with, God-fearing goal-getter.... She noticed that Tommy reached out to her hands.

His gentle touch held her arms as they walked in silence, facing the setting sun.

"What a peaceful place, being with this lovely man," Chloe pondered.

On reflection, physical and material qualities were never what Chloe desired in a man.

She longed to have the love she never had from her father as a child.

She's contented about her conditions and herself, which seemed an irresistible trait.

Not by long chalk influenced by others and their pursuit.

She knew that beauty from within was much more important than from outside.

Chloe's weakness had always been her sheer stubbornness.

Invariably to an extent, it has worked to her advantage.

Especially, dealing with her young life, and the leadership roles she had taken on.

Though, things might be different in relating to aspiring suitors.

Her delicate part had to play the game.

Time flies when one feels lonely.

A year seems like forever. Although Chloe was among other male friends, her feelings for Tommy overshadowed all others.

Supo, her scarred friend, was without fail, kind and gentle with her.

He was always ready to go the extra mile for her. He had shied away from any serious discussion about the future.

Like something was holding him back.

Chloe enjoyed the present with Supo and did not bother about the future.

Chloe set her heart on another.

Communications became fragile by the day between Tommy and Chloe.

The fear of losing him to someone else grew in her mind.

His responses soon moved from absent-mindedness to slight arrogance.

She sensed Tommy felt she was forcing herself on him. Perhaps because studying, living, and marrying someone abroad was every girl's dream.

She felt more confusion than assurance in the words of the Saviour.

Rather than taking it back to Him, she confronted the issues between her and Tommy in a straight line.

One day, Chloe took the bull by the horns, to find out his current disposition towards her.

It was not long before her world came crashing down. Tommy's exact words were,

"Chloe, I see you as my beloved sister; nothing more."

Immediately she read the words as he chatted with her,

she prayed the earth would open and swallow her up.

Like a ghost, she walked out of the café *lifeless*, tears rolling down her cheeks as she walked home.

The good thing was, it was dark and with no light on campus.

No one would notice, once the first tear broke free, the rest followed in an unbroken stream.

A week indoors and alone turned into a month.

By now, Chloe friends became worried about her. She wouldn't talk to anyone about it.

She lost weight and started questioning the very words she 'heard' from the Saviour.

Several voices kept taunting her, reminding her of her failures from childhood.

Most notably, she would not get someone to love her the way she wanted to be cherished.

Chloe longed for her Mama Joe; she was the only person she runs to her world was upside down.

What a vacuum?

She would have told her what to do.

Even though she turned her grievance to the Saviour, it was difficult to hear Him.

She began to lose confidence in her ability to listen to the Saviour's voice.

*"Chloe is drowning,"* she yelled to herself.

Following several attempts to reach his drowning friend, Chuks, her singing partner, spoke with Chloe's siblings about her state.

Sarah, her older sister, later summoned Chloe. After explaining all her misjudgement and actions.

Sarah held her close, saying,

"We all get it wrong, but we are human, in any case.

Sometimes we need to allow the Saviour to work things out and not ourselves."

Tears dropping from Chloe's swollen red eyes, Sarah placed her head on her chest.

"Loved one, I always had imagined you two would end up together."

"Why so?" Chloe inquired; her eyes popped out of her grief.

Sarah smiled, reached out to hold her hands and said. "Mama Joe shared a dream she had with me before she left us. Mama Joe said you ran into her room, pulling Tommy's hands. With great delight, you shouted, Mama! Mama, Tommy asked me to marry him."

"That wouldn't happen now,"

Chloe sighed, tearing streaming down in regret.

Sarah wiped her tears with her hands, continued, "Learning from mistakes and moving on is the best lesson mother's life had taught us.

We must not repeat the same mistakes. We would not allow our fragile hearts to lead us away from trusting the Saviour."

## EPILOGUE

Come unto me, all ye that labour
and are heavy laden,
and I will give you rest.

It wasn't long after Chloe's sister got on her case; Chloe walked back on the road to recovery.

Sarah kept a tab on her and supported fragile Chloe.

Three days later, Chloe heard her bold voice echo from her phone,

"Could you come over and massage my legs?"

Sarah had been recovering from the accident, and she needed all the company she could.

Chloe grumbled as she got out of her bed.

"Yes, sister, " she replied slumberous, "Once the rain stops".

"Are you okay", Sarah asked.

"I would be okay," Chloe spoke straight from the shoulder to her sister.

"You would be fine," Sarah's encouraging voice whispered.

Chloe's wet swollen eyes stared at her old study table mirror.

"This too would pass," she spoke hammer and tongs to herself.

It has been raining cats and dogs all night.

Sometimes, Chloe could not hear herself crying. The rain poured down faster and louder than her tears.

How can it be so hard? Rain is a blessing to some like farmers, and a curse to others when it leads to floods and other forms of devastation.

A friendship that seems so real had in a trice become a source of sorrow.

Chloe rose from the noisy spring bed, with a sharp pain in her stomach.

She had not eaten for the last three days.

Chloe rushed to her fridge for a glass of juice to calm the anxiety surging in her stomach.

A few hours later she was in her sister's place. Sarah, serene, reminded Chloe of all the good things she wanted to forget about Tommy.

For instance, he was among the first few people that had visited her.

She remembered her painful transfer to her hospital.

Tommy visited and stayed every day while she recovered from her injuries.

She spoke about the warm and calm nature that endeared Chloe to him.

If these were not painful enough, she infested her sores

more than ever.

Sarah repeated Mama Joe's dream in which Chloe visited her.

Chloe introduced Tommy to her as her fiancé.

Sarah lost Chloe with stooped shoulders in thought.

Her mind was a million miles away from Sharon's voice.

*"I always deemed that Tommy had an interest in taking their friendship to the next level. Alas, I was wrong! How did this happen? Did I do or say something wrong? The sudden change of direction was shocking to me."*

She knew she had not only messed up her friendship with Tommy but also that things would never be the same again.

Chloe's impatience with the Saviour, and his ability to work out His words, as He did for Jacob His honest intentions, towards Esau was clear.

Could she ever forgive herself? Although it was a hard one, she had learnt her lesson not to take a step without the Saviour's directions.

✿ ✿ ✿

Chloe completed her Tale of Two Cities.

The best and worst times of her life, up to her walk with Tommy with an outburst of tears.

"I wished I did not push; maybe things wouldn't have turned out the way they did."

Mrs Black handed tearful Chloe, a box of tissue, moved her seat slightly while keeping an intense eye on her.

She walked to the table behind Chloe's chair as she sobbed with her sped up breath.

Mrs Black muttered in between her tears.

"Do you want another glass of water?"

"Yes please," cleaning off the condensed congestion

built up in her nose with the fresh tissue from the box.

Mrs Black offered her the glass and spoke softly.

"Chloe, let me first say thank you, for the courage to speak in deep personal details. You should know, even if you had to push Tommy, you did not determine his reaction."

Chloe sighed.

"He chose his reaction, and you should not take responsibility for his actions. Heavens only knows, what had led to his reactions. We would have to wait to find out someday."

Chloe looked at her, smiled with the side of her cheeks.

"I guess I was looking for my happy ending."

It never turned out the way she believed it would.

"I am glad you have been able to express yourself though it had been a harrowing experience. Chloe, do you want to take a break today? I would want you to go home and rest."

Ms Black guided her through the 'waterfall of the Saviour's love'.

She portrayed the love of the Saviour and his intention to man's fallen nature.

The nature described in the self-made image of humanity. Man's self independence and the well of pains caused by man's behaviour.

The counsellor encouraged Chloe to begin a journal to express her feelings.

Ms Black added, picking a copy of her memoir to give her an example.

"You could start from the beginning, your childhood; then trace to the present. Portray your inner needs as an adult."

Chloe looked perplexed at Ms Black's explanations. Yet, a part of her was relieved some of her burdens had lifted.

In a much happy tone, she asked,
"How do I go about this? I am not sure what to put down.
"

"Anything would be fine, picture, mind mapping. You know how to mind map, do you?"

"Yes, I could try."

"I noticed you like poetry. You could write your reflections in the form of poems, song's lyrics, any other form would be a good starting point."

"Okay," Chloe replied with a deep breath.

"I would try to put down some ideas before our next... speaking of, which dates do you have in your diary for me?"

"Two weeks, Tuesday morning, eleven am is free, is this okay for you?"

"Sure, thank you."

Suddenly, it filled Chloe with a sense of severe embarrassment.

*"Someone apart from me knows my deepest insecurity."*

In a panic, she said,

"I have to go now; I feel quite uncomfortable. I would keep in touch. I need to head out."

"Chloe, I understand how you feel."

Ms Black held out her hands, placed over hers and said,

"Can we say a short word of prayer before you leave?"

"Yes, of course, prayer is the key," Chloe replied, smiling.

After Ms Black's prayers, she felt a sense of peace flooding deep inside her.

"Thank you," she voiced with a sincere smile, reflecting the lost dimples in the maze.

"I am hoping to continue my story the next time I am here. Grateful for the time."

"Grateful for the trust," Ms Black replied, walking her to

the door.

"I would look forward to a refreshed Chloe next meeting."

"Definitely! I hope to be back as a refreshed me! Thank you so much," she stepped out of the door walking toward her car, as the setting sun shone into her eyes.

**To be continued in She Smiled – Part 2**

# ABOUT THE AUTHOR

Joan Hephzibah is a mum with two girls and dreams of a gentler life. She holds an HND Quantity Surveyor, BSc Hons in Geography and a Master's degree holder in Health Geography. She had worked with various organisations for several years before picking up her pen to develop her creative skills. She has dealt with personal loss, fears of failures and insecurity in relating with people. These experiences have informed her depiction of a single intelligent lady under pressure to conform to the defined ideals of what relationship means.

Printed in Poland
by Amazon Fulfillment
Poland Sp. z o.o., Wrocław

51258324R00132